Page Intentionally Left Blank

STELLAR CIVILIZATION

STELLAR CIVILIZATION

THE ODD PLANET

C.F. HARRET

Stellar Civilization: The Odd Planet by C.F. Harret

Published by Harret Publishing

The author apologizes for any errors or omissions and would be grateful if notified of any corrections that should be incorporated in future reprints or editions of this book.

Contact information:
Email: cfharret@gmail.com
Instagram: @cfharret
Twitter: @c_harret

ISBN-13: 978-99914-7-536-3 (Kindle eBook)
ISBN-13: 978-99914-7-539-4 (EPUB eBook)
ISBN-13: 978-99914-7-535-6 (Hardcover with dust jacket)
ISBN-13: 978-99914-7-538-7 (Hardcover case laminate)
ISBN-13: 978-99914-7-534-9 (Paperback)

First Edition

Cover design by Primegpx from Fiverr
Edited by Penofadventure from Fiverr

Contents

Part I: Vanessa Hibbs 1

Chapter 1: Glitzing 3

Chapter 2: The Crew 5

Chapter 3: The "Mistake" 11

Chapter 4: A Massive Dung in Space 21

Chapter 5: Miner Number Three 28

Part II: Bobby Brooklyn 33

Chapter 7: The Tunnel 39

Chapter 8: Tripwire 58

Chapter 9: The Magnetic Disturbance 64

Chapter 10: The Encounter 70

Chapter 11: Half-witted 79

Part III: Wendy Dodge 82

Chapter 12: Carrying On 83

Chapter 13: The Lieutenant's Past 96

Chapter 14: Eject 104

Part IV: Nate Kendrick 108

Chapter 15: The Tunnel On the Right 109

Chapter 16: A New Mission 114

Chapter 17: Contemplation 119

Chapter 18: The Octagon 122

Chapter 19: Tough Decision 128

Part V: Erma van Hout 131

Chapter 20: Forty-Four Hours 132

Chapter 21: The Vanishers 150

Chapter 22: Finding Bobby 160

Part VI: Lester Pierce 164

Chapter 23: A Joint Effort 165

Chapter 24: Biting the Dust 171

Chapter 25: Octagonal Twin 176

Chapter 26: The Captain's Plan 181

Chapter 27: The Results 186

ABOUT THE AUTHOR 193

MY GRATITUDE 194

Part I

Vanessa Hibbs

Mining Ship IMS-27506

Chapter 1
Glitzing

I saw how they threw my body in an incinerator, letting the flames scorch it till it turned into a big pile of dark grey ash. This was after they had stuck a needle into the big vein that was on the inner part of my right elbow, allowing a clear liquid to flow in, and subsequently stop me from taking another breath.

I *gave* them permission to do all of that.

I let them do it, not because I wanted to die. It was quite the contrary, I wanted to live. I wanted to see the future and observe how mankind was going to advance itself. The only way that was possible, was through the procedure—the procedure that was going to get my mind into a new vessel. Glitzing it was called, and in my case, that vessel was a ship.

After the glitz, my old body was considered redundant, so that's why they injected it with a fatal dose of euthinazides and threw it in the fire.

I was two hundred and ten years old when the procedure was carried out, and that was exactly seven thousand six hundred and forty years ago, which made me old enough to be tired of being a goddamn ship, and to make matters even more embarrassing, I was a mining ship.

A mining ship was my only option though. It was the cheapest option at that time, and because I was so scared of dying *before* getting a chance to glitz, I immediately signed the contract the moment I had saved enough credits.

I do regret not waiting a bit longer. That way, I could've glitzed into something less degrading. I had heard, however, that the government was going to pass a new law, allowing transfers between vessels. I would cross my fingers if I had any.

But being a mining ship wasn't all that bad, it did have its perks I suppose. You'd get the opportunity to explore the galaxy and didn't have to do any manual labor. Regardless, one does get bored very fast, because everything you did was done routinely. You'd never get the chance to explore the planet itself. You'd just stay in orbit, launch miners, and wait.

We were mining negatanium, a rare powder-like substance used to extract exotic matter, something my hyperdrive used to generate wormholes and keep them from collapsing on themselves. This way we could travel lightyears in mere hours, hyperjumping it was called.

I myself—and by that, I mean my vessel—was powered by dark matter.

My crewmembers, the cognioids, were humans who had glitzed into android-like vessels. They were powered by dense battery packs charged at home, which ultimately got all of its energy from the star. They could also be charged on the ship.

True, mankind has had its struggles in the past, *but* we still managed to survive. We've also inhabited hundreds of planetary systems, and developed technology our ancestors could only dream of.

There weren't a lot of fleshy humans left though, just a couple hundred billion. Most of us had decided to glitz into cognioids or ships, it was safer that way, and you didn't have to worry about food or your health.

But even though we were considered immortal by the majority, you could still die if you lost all of your data without being backed up beforehand.

It happened sometimes.

Chapter 2

The Crew

We were drifting at the edge of a planetary system we had just jumped into. I was mostly surrounded by empty space, with a couple of meteoroids of varied sizes floating here and there. I could barely see the star and the planets from the distance we were at. Zooming in with my telescope would've helped with that, but I didn't see the need for it.

My crewmembers were still in their rectangular-shaped hibernation stations, almost completely powered down, all of them were minutes from waking up.

Lester Pierce, our captain, was the cognioid in the hibernation station at the very right. He was one that did his job very well, always followed protocol, and never let any of his emotions make decisions for him. He was, however, always quite easy to persuade, as long as the protocol wasn't neglected. He had been our captain for about four thousand years.

Next to him we had Erma van Hout, our commander. Family-oriented and a bit too nice if you ask me, I sometimes wondered if she had ever come across any hurdles in her life, because of the massive amounts of positivity she exuded. However, I had seen her throw a tantrum before, so I'd always watched out and tried not to get on her bad side. Next to being overly nice, she was also quite brave, a combination that was pretty rare to see. She had been with us for about five hundred years.

In the station next to Erma's was Lieutenant Nate Kendrick. He was the one I knew the longest and was part of the first crew to ever board on my vessel. Fierce, brutal, and confident to the point of arrogance. A very peculiar personality, that one. He was the one I technically should've trusted the most, because we'd known each other since the very beginning, but I didn't, oddly enough. He was someone that gave me bad vibes, it had been that way since the moment he stepped foot on my vessel and called me bulky. I'm pretty sure I wasn't the only one that felt that way about him.

Next to Kendrick's station was Wendy Dodge, our mechanic. She was the one responsible for anything that needed fixing. She was relatively new to the crew, about two hundred years. She had a very weird taste in music in my opinion. She once played a song about setting the world on fire. *But* she had a great sense of humor, so I guess that evened it out. She has a certain type of masculinity to her, and I always found it kind of attractive.

The last one in the hibernation stations was Bobby Brooklyn. He was the recruit, our newest member, and it was his first mission with us. I didn't know much about him, except that he was the last one of us to get glitzed, think it was six years ago. He didn't even introduce himself when he came onto the ship; just went straight towards the stations, anchored himself onto one, and powered down.

And of course, there was Vanessa Hibbs, that's me! I've already said almost everything about myself, except that I had the best personality out of the whole crew, according to myself. My ship's code was IMS-27506. The IMS stood for Interstellar Mining Ship—very creative, right? The ship itself was made out of cargon, a nearly impenetrable substance. It was painted white, had a matte finish, and to quote the lieutenant, I was admittedly bulky, but that was because I had to carry a lot of negatanium.

If we had mined enough negatanium, we'd bring it back to our appointed refinery back on Earth, which also housed our headquarters. A lot has changed there. Most humans who lived on that ancient planet, were the ones who governed it, the rest were cognioids.

The sun had a Dyson swarm around it, which was made out of trillions of heatproof satellites that harnessed over ninety percent of the star's energy. This powered almost everything in the solar system, and also indirectly charged the battery packs I mentioned.

I wasn't born in the solar system though. I was from Ross 128, a system first inhabited by cognioids only. Humans arrived centuries later because they didn't know how to successfully transport adult humans between systems without killing them, and hyperjumping wasn't a thing back then.

The cognioids did a far better job in Ross 128 than the humans did in the solar system. I know it's not fair to compare the cognioids to humans, because we didn't have problems like hunger and death, but I did expect more from the people I descended from.

Being stored in a machine had other perks as well. You could store as much knowledge as you wanted, as long as you had enough space; you could also delete traumatic life events in a nanosecond—something I know I had done a lot. You could also wave mental illnesses and neurological diseases goodbye because you can get that fixed as well, as long as you didn't change your personality, which was still illegal.

One drawback of being a machine, however, was not knowing if you were being controlled by humans or not. And if we ever get hit by an EMP—something humans invented for reasons I will never know—we'd be done for. Fortunately for us, machines and humans had evolved past violence. Scuffles between humans and machines had never happened.

We were moving through the vast spaces between the meteoroids in the direction of the average-sized star.

When I got past all of the meteoroids, and reached an

even emptier space, the others were just minutes from waking up, so I decided to prep the miners while I still had a bit of time.

To prep the miners, I would turn them on to see if there were any bugs in their system that would prevent them from functioning correctly. They used laser drilling systems to…well, drill. And they used a reverse propulsion system to extract the negatanium. They were quite big, about the same size as two rows of four full-grown humpback whales stacked on top of each other, but the lower end of the miners, where the laser drill was, was the size of a deer. The whole thing looked like a massive funnel with a big lump on top. This was because they needed to store a lot of negatanium ore. Wendy had far more knowledge of the miners than I did, even though they were a part of my vessel. I was just never curious enough to upload all the details into myself.

After two minutes of analyzing, the miners seemed to be functioning well.

I had full control of where I could fly, except when it was on a mining mission. The coordinates would be uploaded beforehand. They did this because ships had hyperjumped to the wrong destinations before and barely made it back with enough dark matter. Sometimes ships didn't make it back at all, and they couldn't even send out message pods for help.

I had five message pods installed in my vessel. They were used sparingly because they used both exotic and dark matter to travel through space, just like any other ship. It was the only way to communicate when we were light years apart from one another.

I used to only have two message pods installed, but I got myself upgraded because I got lost one time and used both of them, one of the scariest moments ever. I still got rescued, but it's an experience I've deleted from my memory, so I can't say much about it. People would sometimes ask me what happened, and I just tell them that I don't know.

Minutes after I was finished prepping the miners, the crew awakened from hibernation. They went into hibernation to save energy and charge up if they needed to. The battery packs they had would last them up to forty-eight hours of continuous use, which might not sound like a lot, but charging to full capacity takes less than five minutes, so that evened it out. You could also upgrade your battery pack to one with more capacity, but nobody on board has done that.

Captain Pierce was the first to release the anchors that were around his wrists and ankles, he pushed himself off of his station and walked into the AVAC, with the others following him once they were up and out of their chambers. AVAC stands for Advanced Vessel Analysis Compartment, and it checked that everything in a cognioid was working properly.

Captain Pierce had the best vessel out of all of us since he upgraded it quite frequently. And so he should've, considering he earned the most credits.

His vessel had dark red detailing in the form of lines with a width of a centimeter. They ran across his arms and legs, around his shoulder plates, breast plates, and even his back plate. The detailing was the same with every cognioid's vessel, except the color. The color differed based on a cognioid's position. Dark red indicated that Pierce was the captain. He was equipped with a lighted steel frame and his body plates were made out of cargon. The frame and plates were the same color on every droid: black.

All cognioids had a humanoid look, without the flesh of course, and they could make the same facial expressions as humans with the help of hundreds of little motors in their face. This was to improve non-verbal communication.

There was no way to distinguish cognioids from one another just by their general appearance because most of them looked the same—apart from the different colored detailing. If you wanted to know who they were, you had to read the name that was engraved on their chest plate to tell them apart from one another, or connect to them wirelessly and check their ID.

Next to the captain's engraved name, was an emblem that all six of us had on our vessel. All cognioids had an emblem next to their engraved names. Although, mine was on the tail of my vessel. Our emblem was a capital M with a pickaxe in the background.

Commander van Hout had dark purple detailing. Her vessel was equipped with a stock frame—which was made out of aluminum—and she had body plates made out of titanium. Besides that, she didn't have any other upgrades.

Lieutenant Kendrick also had a stock frame. His body plates were made out of a gold-cargon alloy, and he had green detailing, with custom tribal prints of the same color—which in my opinion were outdated—on all of his body plates.

Wendy had a cargon frame but with stock body plates. She believed the most important part of a cognioid was the chip where our minds were stored, and that was located in the head, which was part of the frame. She also had a big, bulky right arm with countless tools used by mechanics, standard issue. Her detailing was orange.

Bobby was all stock, and he didn't have a single physical upgrade, not even any upgraded software. I could tell because I received all the non-personal data from the AVAC he was in. He had a light blue detailing on his plates, just like any other recruit.

With everyone awake and fully charged, we were ready to tackle yet another boring mission.

Chapter 3

The "Mistake"

After they were all done in the AVAC, they all walked through the corridor leading to the bridge, and I knew what the captain was going to say, because he'd always give the same weird greeting that only he thought was funny.

"Good space, Vanessa."

Very funny indeed.

"Good day, Captain."

"Have you analyzed the miners yet?"

"Yes, Captain," I answered, while giving a small nod with my holographic body in the middle of the bridge. "They're all functioning normally. We still have ninety-one percent of dark matter left, seventy-five percent of exotic matter, and all cognioids are at full battery capacity."

"Good," he said, and turned away from me to look at the crew who had just entered the bridge.

"Is there anything else you'd like me to do, Captain?" I asked.

"No, Vanessa, that's fine; just notify us when we reach our planet," he said with his back to my hologram. "In the meantime, I'd like to introduce our newest member. Recruit! You're up!"

The recruit seemed startled by the captain's yell, but he quickly shrugged it off and introduced himself.

"Hey everyone, my name is Bobby Brooklyn. I've been assigned to this mission to gain some experience in the field. I hope I can be of great help to all of you."

Recruits would already have all protocols uploaded

into them—along with general information like the blueprints of most weapons etc.—but they still needed to learn how it was in the field. We could upload practical skills, but the field experience is needed to polish those skills.

"Bobby Brooklyn?" the lieutenant asked, confused. "That's a weird name."

"It was generated by a computer," Bobby replied.

Bobby's voice was very high and soft. It sounded like the voice of a teenage kid. I wondered what age he was when he got glitzed. I was about to ask him but someone else beat me to it.

"Tell us more about yourself, kid," Wendy said. "You sound young as hell. What age did you glitz?"

Wendy had a habit of thinking like me. I'd always wanted to bond with her, since she knew my vessel better than I did, but I'd never gotten the chance, even though she's been part of the crew for two hundred years. I always thought we'd make great friends.

"I got glitzed when I was sixteen," Bobby answered. "I had to do it because I had epilepsy, the worst kind. That was six years ago. Since then, I've been working in the refinery. I got promoted last week."

I could immediately feel the energy in the room change after he had said that; it was another tragic story.

"We're very sorry to hear that," I said out of pity.

"It's okay," he replied joyfully. "It feels great not to worry about seizures anymore. And being technically immortal really helps too."

The captain and Wendy started to chuckle and I knew why. Almost everyone was happy right after they were glitzed, thinking all their problems have ended, but what they didn't know was that you start to get very sick of it, and you end up feeling trapped.

"I'll give him thirty years before he starts regretting it," the lieutenant said, legs and arms crossed, leaning against the wall of the bridge next to the corridor.

"Don't listen to him, he's just jealous because you're getting all the attention," the commander added before looking at the lieutenant and shaking her head in disappointment.

"What are you shaking your head for?" the lieutenant asked, annoyed. "The only thing I'm jealous of is him not having to do anything while sitting around watching us do all the hard work."

"So, what you're implying is that you want to do that as well?" the commander asked. "Kind of lazy don't you think?"

"Oh, go suck some dick, Erma," he replied, angry as always. "You're the one that always does the least amount of work around here. Even Vanessa works harder than you."

I didn't know why he had to drag me into the argument. And I was kind of annoyed that he had used my name in the same instance he had used the word dick.

"That's enough," said the captain. "Sometimes I really wonder why I got assigned to you idiots. Get to your stations and do your job. Recruit, feel free to look around, and if there's anything you want to know, just ask."

"Understood, Captain," Bobby replied enthusiastically.

Captain Pierce always knew how to diffuse tension when necessary. He had a strong aversion to conflict. It's weird that he doesn't have a family; he'd make a great member of one, especially with all the fighting that comes with it.

After that little meeting, everyone scattered and went on to do their own thing. The captain and commander were sitting by the only table in the bridge, going over the mission objectives, Wendy left the bridge to tinker with the miners, the lieutenant was going over the map, and Bobby was walking all over the place, trying to learn the things he already had uploaded into him. I kind of liked how peaceful it was. No interruptions, nobody talking, and most importantly, no drama.

After about ten minutes or so, the commander stood up, and excused herself to check on the message pods—she said she needed a distraction. Bobby asked to join her as she walked towards the corridor. She nodded and agreed but gave him a warning.

"Just don't set them off by accident. The exotic matter in them costs more than you will ever make as a mining cognioid."

Bobby nodded and followed her.

As they were walking away and about to turn left into another corridor, the captain shouted at them, "Don't take too long! We still have to go through the mission objectives."

The commander gave a small backwards wave as she went into the corridor.

"Captain?" the lieutenant asked in a confused tone.

"What is it, lieutenant?"

"Wasn't our system supposed to have two stars?"

"I'm not sure," the captain said before turning to my hologram. "Vanessa?"

"I-I don't know, Captain. I'll look into it right away," I stammered.

I quickly looked up the coordinates that were uploaded into me back at HQ and compared it with the ones in our mission objective. I was in disbelief. A mistake like that never happens. I almost thought the lieutenant was playing a cruel joke on me like he usually does, but he was right, the coordinates were different. We were supposed to be in a system with two stars; the system we were in only had one. Someone back at HQ had uploaded the wrong coordinates.

"H-he's right, Captain," I stammered again. "Our objective was on a planet of another system, but these were the coordinates uploaded into me back at HQ."

"Where are we now?" the captain asked.

"I don't know, sir. The coordinates are of a small planet of this system, which seems to be very close to our own solar system, but it's still in uncharted space."

"Fuck!" the captain yelled.

"Do you want me to prep us for the jump to the right system?" I asked.

He paused for a moment, and then said, "No, we've already wasted enough exotic matter. Prep us for the jump back to Earth. We need to report this."

I almost didn't believe what had happened. Mistakes like these were severely frowned upon because of the waste in exotic matter. If only I had double-checked the coordinates before we left Earth.

"I'm sorry, Captain," I said, guilt coursing through my circuit boards.

"It's not your fault, Vanessa, some knucklehead back at HQ must've typed up the wrong coordinates, I bet all my credits that it's a human," he grumbled. "Just prep us for the jump."

"You know," the lieutenant said, "we don't really have to go back just yet."

The captain turned to him. "What do you mean?"

The lieutenant paused for a second, then replied, "If we can find a planet in *this* system with the right conditions, and enough negatanium, we can just mine *that* planet. We won't have to waste any exotic or dark matter to jump home empty handed. Doing that might give a bad impression of you, Captain."

"I'll get demoted if we mine a planet we weren't supposed to," the captain replied. "Along with you, lieutenant."

"Perhaps," the lieutenant replied confidently, "But need I remind you of how people back home feel about wasting exotic matter? Which is worse?"

A silence hit the bridge. The captain knew the

lieutenant was right, even I knew it. Dark and exotic matter were extremely hard to produce, especially the latter. It takes roughly a thousand kilograms of negatanium to make a single gram of exotic matter, and the process takes an entire month.

The captain sighed, "I'm sure they'll understand."

Cognioids didn't breathe or need oxygen, but we did sigh sometimes because it was a habit engraved in our personality.

The lieutenant shook his head, "I'm pretty sure they won't, Captain. Don't get me wrong, I'd love to see you taint your reputation, but not when it also concerns mine."

"Don't worry, I'll take full responsibility," the captain replied.

The lieutenant shrugged his shoulders. "Alright, if you say so."

"Captain?" I asked.

The captain turned and looked my hologram straight in the eyes, even though that wasn't how I saw him. "Yes, Vanessa?"

"I think there is a way we could make the lieutenant's plan work without any of us getting in trouble."

"And how would we do that?" the captain asked.

Just as I was about to tell him my plan, the commander and Bobby walked in.

"Okay, we're back," the commander said. "Did me and the recruit miss anything while we checked the pods?"

"Oh, nothing much," the lieutenant replied. "Except that we're in the wrong system!"

The commander tilted her head, confused. "What do you mean wrong system?" she asked. "Where are we now?"

She immediately turned to the captain for an answer, thinking the lieutenant was making an unfunny joke like he always did.

The captain turned to her as well and said, "Uncharted space."

"What!?" she yelled. "How did this even happen?"

"We don't know," the captain said. "But there's a pretty good chance it might be an error from back home. Wrong coordinates were uploaded into Vanessa."

"And what now?" the commander asked. "Do we go back home?"

"We haven't decided yet," said the captain. "Vanessa was about to tell us a plan she had."

Right as I was about to attempt to explain my plan a second time, Bobby intervened with a raise of his hand. "Uhm, shouldn't we wait for the mechanic?"

The captain nodded. "Yes, you're right," he said. "I'll send her a message. We'll wait for her to join us before Vanessa tells us her plan."

Everybody was quiet for a minute as we waited for Wendy. It felt like we we're all thinking the same thing: how the fuck did something like this happen?

"It's weird," the commander said. "I've never heard of something like this happening."

"Might be human error," the captain said.

"Computer errors are rare, but they do happen," Bobby added.

The lieutenant chuckled. "Or maybe it was done with a *motive*," he said, while making his fingers dance in front of the commander's face.

"Don't," the commander replied, knocking away his hands and putting her hand on her head, as if she was mentally exhausted. "Just don't start with your conspiracies, Nate."

"Don't call me Nate!" the lieutenant shouted. "We're not that close."

The commander sighed. "Whatever."

The next moment, we heard a loud clunking sound coming closer towards us and very fast. It was Wendy and she was running.

She entered the room. "I came as fast as I could," she

said. "What the hell do you mean by wrong system? Where are we now?"

The captain shook his head. "Okay, I can't explain this again," he said. "You want to take this one, Kendrick?"

The lieutenant turned to Wendy, arms crossed. "You know," he added, with a smirk on his face, "you're cute when you're confused."

"Just shut it, and tell me what happened," Wendy shouted angrily.

The lieutenant chuckled. "And she's back!"

Wendy shook her head and squinted her robotic eyes. "Dude," she said. "Stop!"

Everybody—including me—looked at the lieutenant, failing to understand why he would be joking in this situation. He looked at all of us with small hint of guilt in his expression.

"Fine," he said, as he rolled his eyes. "Something went wrong before we left Earth. Vanessa had the wrong coordinates uploaded into her. We're currently in uncharted space."

Wendy immediately turned to the captain, locking eyes with him. "Human?" she asked with a poker face, but clearly joking.

"The only logical explanation in my opinion."

"So, what now?" she asked

"The lieutenant's plan was to find and mine a nearby planet," the captain said. "Vanessa was about to explain how we could make that work, without any of us getting into trouble."

"Alter the logs," Wendy said instantly, with a small shrug of her shoulders, indicating that it was the obvious next choice. "How else would we be able to make that work?"

"Exactly!" I shouted. "If we change the logs, saying that we went to the system we were supposed to go to, they'll never find out."

It was a foolproof plan. We find a planet nearby, with enough negatanium to mine, take what we can, change the coordinates in our logs to the one we should've gone to, and go back to HQ, nobody would know.

"But..." Bobby began, raising one of his hands. "What if someone rats us out?"

Everyone immediately stood still, knowing that was a possibility, but there was only one person on the crew who would do such a thing, and we all knew who that was, so everybody—except Bobby—turned to the lieutenant and stared at him.

"Damn it!" he shouted. "It was my plan from the start!" he added angrily. "I'll get in trouble too if they find out, you know." He followed with a deep sigh. "Sometimes you guys make me want to exchange to a different team."

"Be my guest," Wendy said.

"Fine!" the lieutenant replied, "When we get back to HQ, I'll submit an application for an exchange. We'll see how this team holds up after I'm gone"

Wendy let out a small chuckle, right before high fiving the commander. It seemed as if they wanted to show the lieutenant that they were plotting a way to get him to leave the team, and they had now succeeded.

"Damn," I said. "I wish I had arms to high five you guys."

The lieutenant turned to my hologram with a shocked expression. "Vanessa..." he said, "We've known each other since the beginning."

I felt kind of guilty after he said that. He was right. Out of everyone in the room, I had known him the longest, but he did get on my nerves sometimes.

"We're just messing with you," I said, trying to make him feel better. "Nobody wants you to switch teams."

Wendy raised her hand and looked at everyone. "I do."

"That's enough!" the captain shouted. "We need to

focus on the problem."

Even though I wasn't very fond of the lieutenant, I felt bad for him. I always thought that there was something wrong with his personality. I figured he had a traumatizing human life, but he never talked about his past; nobody except him knows his story.

"Are there any suitable planets in this system, Vanessa?" the captain asked.

"I'm scanning right now."

"Good, let us know when you've found one," the captain said as he walked away. "The rest of you can go back to work. We'll meet up on the bridge once Vanessa is done scanning."

At the captain's order, everybody went back to doing their jobs. Wendy went back to the miners, the commander and the captain were sitting at the table again, with Bobby behind them on his metal toes, trying to see what they were doing, and the lieutenant went into one of the cabins to lay on a bed, hurt by our comments.

Chapter 4

A Massive Dung in Space

I had to scan every planet on this system, which wasn't hard, but it did take a bit of time. There were a lot of factors to consider when looking for a mineable planet. The first and most important is its gravitational force. Cognioids can withstand a much higher gravitational force than humans, but we still prefer one below 2.0G. Anything higher might damage a cognioid's vessel. A high gravitational force also made it more difficult for our miners to take off from the surface.

A second important factor is the temperature on the planet. Too hot and some components might melt, too cold and a cognioid could actually freeze and be unable to move.

And let's not forget the substance the planet is made out of. That's important. We can't land on gas planets.

The system we were in seemed to have nine planets, most of which were not suitable for the miners or cognioids to land on. There were, however, two planets that seemed to meet the requirements we needed to get closer to see if they had negatanium, my sensors couldn't pick up the radiation of negatanium ore from the distance we were at.

It took about an hour for us to get close enough. It seemed like an ordinary system, which made it weirder that nobody had ever charted this area, especially considering how close it was to the solar system. From the two suitable planets, one was in the habitable zone, the other one was a bit too far.

I really wonder who uploaded the incorrect coordinates. It was one of the most important, and also one of the simplest, tasks to do—even for a human. I wouldn't want to be the person that had made such a mistake. Whoever it was had wasted exotic matter, dark matter, and quite a bit of time. Luckily, for that person, we were making the effort not to go back empty-handed.

It wasn't a bad idea to mine a planet without authorization. Yes, we might get in trouble if we got caught. However, if we come back from an unauthorized mining mission and bring back negatanium, the repercussions won't be nearly as severe. Kendrick fit the definition of an evil genius perfectly.

And, like I said, Captain Pierce was quite easy to persuade. Although he did have his limits, he doesn't say no often. When he does, you know it's something serious.

I was getting a negatanium reading from both planets. The one in the habitable zone seemed to give a stronger signal, which, of course, indicated more negatanium.

I activated my hologram again in the middle of the bridge, calling the captain.

He stood up, stopping whatever he was doing with the commander, and walked towards me. The commander and Bobby followed him. "Done scanning already?" the captain asked.

"Yes, Captain."

"I'll send a message to the others. Is it good news?"

"Yes, Captain."

"Great."

Captain Pierce always had this cool demeanor to him. It was hard to explain. He always cut to the chase, but not in an arrogant or intimidating way. I understood why he was appointed captain.

I, myself, could never be a captain. I liked to follow orders rather than give them. I think it's because I know I wouldn't be able to handle the responsibility.

After the captain sent the message to the others, it took about ten minutes before the lieutenant showed up, Wendy following closely behind.

"So, any good news?" she asked as she strolled into the bridge.

"Yes." I replied. "There are two planets in this system that are giving off a decent amount of negatanium radiation. Both meet the requirements for landing and mining, but I'm getting a stronger signal from the planet in the habitable zone."

"Great, that means the temperature will be better," the lieutenant said. "So, we choose that one."

That's when I noticed something strange from the data.

"There's something else," I said.

"What is it?" the captain asked.

"The wrong coordinates that were uploaded into me…are of this exact planet."

Everybody stood still.

"Okay," the lieutenant said, breaking the awkward silence. "I was kidding before when I said it was done with a motive, but now it seems very likely."

The commander turned to the captain. "Do you think someone back on Earth *wants* us to mine this planet?"

"I don't know," the captain said. "And I don't know how I should feel about it either."

"I say we mine it anyway," the lieutenant said. "It could still be a coincidence, and nothing bad can happen from mining it. It'll be like any of our other missions."

The captain looked around seeing if anyone else had something to say. "Any objections?"

Nobody said a word.

"It's settled then. We'll mine the one in the habitable zone. Vanessa, release the scouters to evaluate the planet once we're close enough."

"Yes, Captain."

Scouters were small saucer-like machines that gave a more detailed analysis of a planet. They analyzed the atmosphere, the geological makeup, the best site for landing, and which area had the most negatanium. I was equipped with thousands of them, it could take anywhere from a couple of hours to an entire day to analyze the planet, but once we had found a good landing site with enough negatanium, we can land the miners there and wait. None of the cognioids would have to land on the planet if everything went smoothly.

Right after the captain instructed me, I started releasing all of the scouters from the underside of my vessel, causing them to deploy like a swarm of bees defending their home.

All we had to do was wait.

"It'll take approximately one to ten hours for the scouters to finish analyzing the planet," I said.

"Alright," the commander replied. "Can you bring up an image of the planet, Vanessa?"

I deactivated the hologram of myself and brought up a colorized holographic image of the planet which I had rendered after scanning the planet superficially.

"That is one ugly ass planet," the lieutenant added.

"You're right," said the commander. "Kind of reminds me of you."

The lieutenant rolled his eyes. "Who cares what I look like. I haven't given a rat's ass about my appearance since I was twenty-five."

"Let yourself go at such a young age huh?" Wendy said. "Was it 'cause of a lady?"

The lieutenant scoffed and raised his middle finger towards Wendy. "Piss off."

Wendy chuckled and turned to the hologram. "I do have to agree though; this planet isn't much of a looker."

The planet being ugly was quite the understatement,

and I'd seen quite a decent number of ugly planets. There was no sign of water, it had too many craters to my liking, the atmosphere—something the scouters still had to analyze—didn't seem like the type humans would like to live in, and the color was the worst one a planet could ever have: dark brown. It made it look like a massive pile of dung orbiting through space.

"The way it looks couldn't matter less," the captain said. "We're just here for the negatanium."

"Will we be stepping foot on it?" Bobby asked.

Wendy turned and looked at him with one of her metal eyebrows raised. "What?" she asked, with a confused tone to her voice. "Don't you have the protocols uploaded into you?"

"I-I do…" Bobby stuttered, "but I thought it'd be fun if we explored an uncharted planet."

Wendy looked around for a second to see if anybody was going to tell him. When nobody said anything, she turned to Bobby and said, "Only if the situation requires it, buddy. We're not here to have fun."

"Sorry…" Bobby replied.

"No need to say sorry, kid," the commander added. "We were all recruits once, except for Vanessa of course. She started out as a ship."

I kind of felt bad when she said that. I was already sick and tired of being a ship, I didn't need to be reminded that I'd been one since the start.

"Thanks," I said sarcastically.

The commander immediately noticed my frustration and apologized. "I'm sorry. I didn't mean it like that, Vanessa."

"It's okay."

"It's nothing to feel insecure about," she said. "And hey, if the government passes that law, you'll be able to transfer yourself into a cognioid."

I thought about what she said for a moment and

replied, "And become the new captain of this team?"

"See, that's the spirit."

"What'll happen to the old captain then?" the captain asked.

"K-I-A, most likely," said the lieutenant, chuckling.

Wendy approached the lieutenant, put her hand on his shoulder, and looked him straight in the eyes. "Along with our lieutenant," she teased him.

The lieutenant scoffed and slapped away Wendy's hand. "Need I remind you that mechanics are the ones most likely to get lost on a planet."

He was right. Mechanics are the ones that go on the surface the most, usually to fix the miners if something went wrong. That's why Wendy was constantly checking on them, to prevent any problems when they *do* land on the surface so she wouldn't have to go down there.

"Like I care," Wendy replied. "I got myself backed up before boarding the ship."

That's when Bobby gasped and looked at everyone with his eyes wide open, as if he had made a terrible mistake. "Shit!" he yelled, surprising everyone with his language. "I forgot to back myself up!"

A roar of laughter escaped the lieutenant's mouth. "Better send out a message pod then, recruit!" he shouted and gave Bobby a slap on his back.

"It's not funny! If something happens to me on this mission, my glitzing would have been for nothing! All those credits will have gone to waste."

The lieutenant continued laughing, but gradually came to a halt. "Don't worry, kid, a recruit getting killed in action rarely happens, and let's not forget, you're not a mechanic." He then looked at Wendy with a grin on his face.

Wendy rolled her eyes at the lieutenant. "Funny," she said.

"Why thank you, Wendy."

"Okay, that's enough," the commander said. "Go

back to work, and let the scouters do their job."

Everybody stayed quiet for a second, then scattered again to do their own thing—not that there was a lot to do. Almost everything on the ship was automated. The only person with a real job was Wendy. She actually had to do manual labor. The rest of the crew—including me—only had to read and analyze data and discuss it with each other.

I did nothing but gaze upon the emptiness of the system we were in while we waited for the scouters to do their job. The only thing I could see clearly without using a telescope was the dark brown planet—because we were so close to it—and the yellow star it was orbiting around.

Chapter 5

Miner Number Three

The commander entered the bridge after some time, the rest of the crew already present. I could see from the commander's body language that she was annoyed, probably because she too was bored of having nothing to do.

"Vanessa," she said, "have you gotten the analysis of the atmosphere yet?"

"Yes, Commander," I replied, as the rest of the crew abandoned whatever they were doing and gathered around my hologram. "It seems to be composed of fifty percent nitrogen, twenty-two percent carbon dioxide, eighteen percent carbon monoxide, five percent argon, three percent oxygen, and two percent methane."

The commander raised both of her metal eyebrows, looking surprised. "Interesting," she said. "Doesn't seem like a bad place to terraform. What's the temperature?"

"Fifty degrees Celsius at its hottest and minus twenty-two at its coldest."

"Not bad," the commander said. "I think it would be wise to give the terraforming division a hint that there might be a suitable planet for them in this system."

The lieutenant looked at her and shook his head. "What's wrong with you!?" he shouted. "Do you want to get caught?"

"We don't have to tell them personally," she replied. "We could just send them an untraceable, anonymous message."

The lieutenant sighed, and shook his head again, this time out of disbelief. "That's not going to work, there isn't a single organization or government entity that responds to anonymous messages, let alone untraceable ones. They will think it's a prank."

Just as the commander was going to say something, Bobby intervened, raising his hand. "What if we give them a message on paper, instead of a digital one?" he asked. "Maybe that will get their attention."

"Nice thinking, recruit," the commander added. "What do you think, Captain?"

The captain paused, and didn't say a thing, even his face was expressionless. He didn't look at anybody, but instead stared at the ground, as if he was thinking very deeply. "We'll talk about it when we're finished with mining."

"I'm telling you, we'll all end up getting caught and demoted," the lieutenant said.

That's when I got an alert from one of the scouters. It had found an area with a good amount of negatanium and it had a flat surface and good weather. Perfect for the miners to land.

"Captain," I said.

He stopped looking at the ground and turned to my hologram.

"The scouters have found a suitable mining area," I continued, and brought up the holographic map, showing the location. "Should I release the miners?"

"Yes," he replied. "Go ahead."

I opened up all five hangers that housed a miner, and one by one they shot out of my vessel, entered the atmosphere, landed on the appointed area, and started to drill. The whole process took less than ten minutes.

"How long will it take for them to reach full capacity?" Bobby asked.

I turned my holographic body towards him. "About twelve hours, give or take."

The mining area was on the northern part of the

planet. The negatanium wasn't too deep, so it wouldn't take long for the miners to reach it. But about two minutes after the miners activated their laser drills, one of them stopped drilling.

"Guys?" I called. "There seems to be a problem with one of the miners."

"What do you mean?" the captain replied.

I switched the hologram to that of the third miner. The drilling system was highlighted red, and blinking.

"It's the laser drill from miner number three," the commander added. "It appears to have malfunctioned."

Wendy kicked the only table in the bridge. It was bolted to the ground, causing a deafening clunking sound. "Fuck!" she yelled. "I checked that one three fucking times! It didn't show any problems."

The captain sighed. "Is it the same one that was acting up last time?"

"It appears so, Captain."

The captain turned to Wendy. "I guess you're up."

Wendy put a hand on her forehead, and closed her eyes, shaking her head in frustration. "Great. Just fucking great."

"And Vanessa?"

"Yes, Captain?"

"Report this miner when we're back at the refinery."

"Noted."

Wendy walked towards Bobby. She grabbed him firmly by his shoulder, startling him, and asked, "You still up for stepping foot on this planet, recruit?"

"You can call me Bobby," he replied. "And no thanks." He grabbed Wendy's arm, slowly raised it off of his shoulder, and dropped it next to him. "There's no way I'm going down there without being backed up."

"Come on," Wendy said playfully. "There's no need to be scared. We'll fix the miners and get back on the ship in no time. Who knows when you'll get another chance to explore a planet during a mission, let alone an uncharted one."

"She's right, kid," the lieutenant added. "The last time I landed on a planet during a mission was at least fifty years ago. I'd take the chance if I were you."

Bobby shook his head. "Nice try, but it's still a no."

"How about this," Wendy said. "If something happens to you, I'll take your mind chip and upload it into a new vessel. I'll even pay for it."

Bobby looked at Wendy, arched one of his eyebrows, and asked, "What if my chip gets destroyed as well?"

Wendy turned and looked at the commander and lieutenant. "See, that's why it's smart to upgrade your frame to a stronger one."

The commander looked at Wendy, giving her the same look Bobby had given her. "There's nothing wrong with having a stock frame."

"The commander is right, kid," the lieutenant said. "Stock frames are more than enough to protect you. I've never heard of someone with a stock frame damaging their chip."

"Anyway," Wendy added. "Last chance to join me." She pointed to the hologram of the miner. "You in or you out?"

Bobby looked at the captain. "What do you think, Captain?"

"I think it's your decision to make," he replied.

"Okay, fine," Bobby said. "I'm in, but only if you promise to recover my mind chip if anything happens."

"Promise, but I'll only pay for half of your new vessel."

"You said you'd pay for everything."

"No, that's not what I said. I said I'd pay for it. I didn't say how much I'd pay."

Bobby rolled his eyes, "Fine. Let's do this."

It always surprised me how Wendy and the lieutenant

were so good at convincing people to do something. They seemed so manipulative at times; it made me wonder what they had been like as humans.

After that little conversation, Bobby and Wendy left the bridge and headed towards the landers, those were pods that could enter and leave a planet using dark matter, I had six of them on my vessel.

I started to feel envious, because I really wanted to join them, it was moments like these that made me regret not saving more credits at the end of my life as a human. The only planets I had ever landed on were already colonized. There was no adventure in that.

As a ship, I had had the chance to save more than enough for countless glitzes. The only thing that was holding me back was that stupid law. What was the point of gaining immortality if it meant you'd end up losing your freedom? It made me angry just thinking about it.

I could see Bobby and Wendy entering a lander through one of the cameras in the corridor—which I had installed all around my vessel. They didn't have to wear or bring anything, because why would they? They were cognioids that didn't breathe, and Wendy had everything they needed to fix the miner in that arm of hers.

Even though I felt envious of the two, I still hoped the best for them, and didn't want anything bad to happen, especially not to the unbacked up Bobby.

Part II

Bobby Brooklyn

The Recruit

Chapter 6

The Surface

The lander trembled as it entered the atmosphere, which didn't help at all with the dreadful situation I had put myself in. It was my own fault anyway. I was the one that got all excited and asked if it was allowed to step foot on the planet.

It was a shame that cognioids couldn't rely on breathing techniques to calm themselves down. I could've really used it.

You would think that glitzing yourself into a machine would rid you of any kind of emotion, especially fear, but no, they didn't allow that. Emotions were part of our personality; it was what differentiated us from other types of machines. But I knew one thing for sure: I was going to delete this ride from my memory the moment the mission was over.

I kept telling myself that I needed to relax, that nothing bad was going to happen, it was just fixing one of the miners, and I didn't even have to do anything. I just had to watch Wendy do all the work—who, by the way, seemed to be handling it pretty well. And of course she was; she was a mechanic after all. They stepped foot on planets more than any other cognioid.

As the lander was halfway to reaching the surface, I didn't have anything to look at but Wendy. Her eyes were closed and she seemed very calm and collected, sitting still with her arms resting beside her vessel, as if she was meditating. I couldn't help but wonder what her story was, she had a certain ruggedness to her. Masculine, but with a feminine twist. It was a peculiar combination, but it suited her.

The screen in the lander displayed the time that was left until we'd reach the surface. One minute, which might not sound like a long time, but it sure felt like it. And to make matters worse, it was completely silent—aside from the noise caused by the trembling of the lander of course—and that silence made everything in the lander awkward for me.

We got pretty lucky though. To find not one, but two planets right next to each other that contained negatanium? That didn't happen every day. Negatanium wasn't a substance you'd find just anywhere.

The negatanium we mined wasn't for a company—those didn't exist anymore—it was for the government. Everything was owned and managed by them. It made everything more orderly and efficient. We did get paid though, quite a good sum of credits too. I would be paid the least out of everyone, of course, because I'm new. But I'd get a raise in my salary every year, which was great, because that would get me closer to my goal: owning a non-sentient spaceship.

My dream was to explore the uncharted parts of the galaxy alone—after getting myself backed up, of course.

I still couldn't believe I hadn't thought of doing that. If anything happened that damaged my mind chip, I'd be done for.

As we reached the surface, the trembling of the lander increased for a brief second, then suddenly came to a halt when it touched down and deactivated the boosters. The hatch from the lander opened upwards, and the brown-colored atmosphere started to displace into the lander. Even tardigrades wouldn't be able to handle this.

After pushing the over-the-shoulders restraints off, I followed Wendy out of the lander, taking a step out of the door and putting my feet on the solid, dry ground. The whole surface was dark brown, even more so than what it looked like from the bridge.

"This one is definitely in my top ten," Wendy said.

I felt a wave of relief at finally hearing her speak after that hellish silence in the lander.

"Top ten?" I asked.

"Of the ugliest planets I've visited."

I let out a small chuckle. "Have you seen worse?"

"Yeah," she answered. "Earth is one of them"

I was certain that she was kidding. To me, Earth was the best looking planet out of every planet that we had colonized. It was extremely well-developed and had the most beautiful monuments in human history.

I laughed awkwardly, thinking it was a joke.

"I wasn't joking," she said.

"I don't understand."

"I wouldn't expect you to."

"Bad experiences?"

She walked away from me, heading towards miner number three, I didn't know what else to do but follow her.

"No," she said, still walking. "I just find the humans there repulsive. Every planet that humans have colonized becomes a factory. It's so lifeless."

"Well, it's necessary, don't you think?"

"How so?"

"To advance the human race."

"Ah, so you're one of *those* people."

"I mean, if it weren't for our need to excel, we'd never be able to glitz ourselves into cognioids."

"True, I suppose. I just see it in a different way."

"Care to explain?"

"No. You're too young to understand, anyway. I'll tell you when you get older."

I took offence to that. Twenty-two was more than old enough if you asked me, but I didn't want to start an argument with her, considering she was my superior.

I did, however, wonder what had led her to that mindset against Earth. I had always admired the human race for what it had achieved with its tiny brain. I wouldn't have been able to survive my illness if it weren't for those achievements.

We had landed a couple of meters next to the faulty miner, which had landed perfectly balanced, but I didn't see the laser drill working. I thought there might have been a gravel stuck in the drilling mechanism—something I had never seen in my life—but the information that was uploaded into me said that gravel was the most common cause of a faulty laser drill.

Wendy crawled under the miner to investigate, and after two minutes of clinking and clunking, I could hear her muffled voice. "Just as I thought, gravel stuck in the drilling mechanism."

I felt kind of proud of myself for having guessed it right, and on my first day as well.

"Is it a big piece?" I asked.

"Nah, not really. I can pick it away with my tweezer."

She retracted her hand from her mechanic's arm, and out came a pair of tweezers. She reached deep into the drilling mechanism and removed a small piece of gravel the size of a peanut.

"Hey, Wendy?" I asked, as she came out from under the miner.

"Yes?"

"Were you always like this?"

"Huh?" she looked confused and frowned at me. "What do you mean?"

"Well…I know you're a female, but you still exude a kind of male aura. Are you—?

"Gay?" she finished my question abruptly.

I nodded.

Wendy started to giggle as she changed the tweezers

back to her hand. "I get that a lot," she said. "But no, I'm not gay. It's just my personality. Not all gay people have traits of both sexes."

"Sorry," I replied

"It's fine, kid," she said. "But there is someone on our crew that's gay. I'm not telling you who it is, you'll figure it out on your own."

That made me curious. None of the others really struck me as gay, but to be fair, I had a really bad sense of whether someone was gay or not. In my life, I had never met someone who *was*, seeing as I spent most of my time in a hospital. And even though I befriended a lot of healthcare workers, we weren't *that* close.

I walked closer to the miner, and bent down to look at the underside of the drill, but it hadn't started yet. "How long till the miner is ready to drill?" I asked.

"I've removed the piece of gravel, but I need to restart the whole system," Wendy said as she walked to the other side of the miner and opened up a cap. It was the miner's manual terminal. "Might take half an hour or so. You can go look around if you want. Maybe you'll learn something from this planet."

What was there to learn? Everything seemed so dull here. The only interesting thing about the planet were the colossal craters in the far horizon. The edges made them look like mountains from where I was standing, which was kind of neat, but they were just for looking; we weren't allowed to go that far.

The starlight barely made it through the brown clouds of the atmosphere, which gave the planet an eerie overcast look. The sky that wasn't covered by the clouds was pure red, like oxygen-saturated blood.

A small shiver moved through my vessel as I gazed at the sky. It was a weird feature added by the engineers, to make us feel more human.

Chapter 7

The Tunnel

As I waited for the miner to get going again, I wondered what the rest of the crew was up to. We were able to communicate through old fashioned radio waves, but I didn't want to disturb them and risk coming off as the new guy who was starving for attention.

I couldn't wait to go back home and tell my family I had explored an uncharted planet on my first day. I was from a planet of the Ross 128 system, and I still lived with my parents, both of whom were still human, and planning to glitz at the end of their lives.

If there was one thing that I missed the most about being human, it was being able to taste my mother's cooking. Unfortunately for me, cognioids didn't eat food, let alone taste it. We did have the ability to activate the part of our mind that allowed us to relive an experience, including tastes and smells, but it wasn't the same.

There was this one dish my mother used to make. It was an ancient recipe. The dish had fried eggplant in it, but that's all I knew of it. I had never learned the recipe or even what it was called. Perhaps that was something I should do when I got back home, considering I basically had unlimited memory as a cognioid.

"Wendy, Bobby," the captain said through the radio. "There's something important we need to talk about."

The quality of the transmission wasn't that great. We could hear the captain clearly, but there was a lot of background noise. I figured it was the result of the thick brown clouds above us.

Wendy was still working behind the miner's terminal as she replied, "Don't tell me another miner malfunctioned."

"No, it's one of the scouters," the captain replied.

"You know I can't fix scouters, Captain," she said. "We leave them on the planet after every mission. You know this."

"It's not that…" the captain began.

"Then what is it?"

"Wendy, it found something."

Wendy stopped working on the faulty miner. "What do you mean it found something? Like another mining site?"

"No," the captain answered. "There looks to be an artificial tunnel a couple of kilometers from you guys."

Wendy and I looked at each other, and just stood there, not knowing what to say, as if we were frozen like two sculptures. Surely the captain was joking.

"But I thought you guys said this was uncharted space?" Wendy asked.

That's when Vanessa chimed in, the quality of the transmission got even worse at that point. "It is," she said. "I have the latest information from the database, updated last week."

"Is it really an artificial one, or just a natural phenomenon?" Wendy asked.

"We're not entirely sure, it looks too symmetrical to be natural, and it goes deep underground. Too deep for the scouters to analyze," Vanessa replied.

"This *can't* be a coincidence," Wendy said. "Wrong coordinates uploaded onto a mining ship that leads to an uncharted negatanium-rich planet that has an *artificial* tunnel?"

"I know," the captain said. "Something doesn't feel right. We'll add this in our debriefing when we get back to Earth, but for now, we are obligated to investigate it."

It was unreal. Artificial tunneling in an uncharted territory could mean one thing, and one thing only: alien life!

In all of human history, alien life had never been discovered.

If we were to find something, it would put us in the history books—something I also dreamed about. But I didn't want to get ahead of myself. We still had to investigate the tunnel. There's a chance it is just a natural phenomenon.

This was something I absolutely *had* to experience, regardless of whether I had been backed up or not. Anyone who had found any sign of alien life would be regarded as a hero.

"Alright, I guess we'll have to go take a look," Wendy said. "Are any of you guys up there going to join us down here?"

"Me," came the manly, menacing voice through the clouded transmission. It was the lieutenant. "I'm coming down soon with the weapons."

Wendy turned to me and grabbed me by the shoulder, giving me a small shake "It's your lucky day kid!" she said. "Experiencing something like this, and on your first day too. It's unheard of."

"I-I know!" I stammered with enthusiasm. "I'm kind of excited."

She let go of my shoulder, and looked me in the eyes. "But seeing how you aren't backed up, do you still want to join us?" She smirked.

I nodded. "Yeah, it's fine. I'd be quite a fool if I passed up an opportunity like this. Just promise me you'll recover my mind chip if something bad happens."

She nodded. "Sure thing," she said. "Not going to lie though, you've got more backbone than I expected. I wasn't like you as a recruit."

"Thanks, I suppose."

She turned and walked back to the miner's terminal and got back to work. "We just have to wait for the lieutenant and the weapons now. Have you ever used a plasma ray before?"

I shook my head, even though she couldn't see me.

"No, but I know what it is and how to use it. It's in one of the protocols I have uploaded."

"Alright. Do you want the plasma ray or the plasma cannon?"

"The ray is fine."

A plasma ray had less power to it than the cannon, but it was still pretty powerful. Plasma rays were carried by hand, and cannons were put on the shoulder. We weren't allowed to kill or maim any alien life form, should we encounter any, but we were allowed to defend ourselves if we were attacked.

Our protocols stated that we had to investigate anything that was suspected to be of alien origin. If the tunnels clearly seemed artificial or if we'd encounter any life form, we had to report back to HQ immediately with a message pod. There had been numerous occasions where crews had suspected the presence of alien life or had encountered remnants of it, but they were all revealed to be false accounts. The crews that reported the encounters were shunned by everyone for wasting resources, so we needed to be one hundred percent sure before about the presence of alien life before we sent a message pod to the higher ups.

For over two hundred thousand years, after visiting countless planets, not one single sign of alien life had been discovered, and every century that passed made us believe more and more that Earth was the only place in the universe where life had formed.

"Okay," the lieutenant said over the radio. "I'm entering the lander now, I'll be landing twenty-six meters north of your lander, don't stand in the way if you don't want to get crushed."

"If anything happens unexpectedly, follow protocol," the captain transmitted.

"Good luck, guys," the commander added. "And be sure to make it back safe."

And lastly, Vanessa chimed in, "Good luck!"

Both me and Wendy said, "Thanks."

It was kind of nice the way they cared about our safety. This was the first interstellar crew I had worked with and I had expected them to be strict and uncaring.

"Bobby," I heard the captain call me. "Seeing how you didn't back yourself up, you can always stay at the mining site or come back up, it's your call, we'll understand."

"It's fine, Captain," I replied. "I already told Wendy this is a once in a lifetime opportunity."

"That's what I like to hear. If everything goes well, know that a very good evaluation is waiting for you back on the ship."

"Thanks, Captain."

I was excited. I couldn't wait to go back home after the mission and see the look on my friends' faces when I tell them I was part of a tunnel exploration team on an uncharted planet.

It did, however, make me kind of anxious. If something were to fall on my head and break my chip, I was as good as dead.

A couple of minutes later, the lieutenant touched the ground, and stepped out of his lander.

If I could've chosen someone to explore the tunnels with, it wouldn't have been him. I know I had only known him for less than a day, but he rubbed me the wrong way. He gave me a weird feeling, you know? Almost as if he'd use the plasma cannon—which was attached to his left shoulder—on me, just for fun.

"Is everything alright, kid?" he asked me. "You're staring at me like you want to pounce on me."

I immediately turned away because he had startled me, but then I looked at him again. I gave him a small nod. "Sorry, Lieutenant. I was just thinking about something else and happened to be looking your way."

"Alright then," he added. "I brought down three

plasma rays and three plasma cannons, which one do you want?"

"The plasma ray."

"Give me the cannon," Wendy said.

He handed us each what we asked for and put the rest in a bag he was carrying around his free shoulder. "I'll keep the others in my bag, just to be safe. If your weapon runs out, tell me, okay?"

"Do you think we'll have to use it down there?" I asked.

The lieutenant didn't respond, he didn't even look at me. Instead, he looked up and said, "Vanessa, you can send down the rover now."

"Just released it, it'll be down in a minute," Vanessa responded.

The rover was, well, a rover. It ran on a battery like our vessels; it had its own lander, which could also exit the atmosphere, and it had about a thousand kilometers of range. I had never ridden in one, but I knew all about it because of the protocols.

I looked up at the sky and zoomed in. I could see the rover's lander entering the atmosphere. It looked like a small orange fireball, barely visible against the red sky. It looked as if it was a small meteor that was about to strike the planet.

The lieutenant was also staring at it, but after a couple of seconds he turned and looked at Wendy who was installing the plasma cannon on her left shoulder. "You ever been investigating suspected alien artifacts?"

"Nope, first time. You?

"First time as well," the lieutenant replied. "You think we'll actually find something?"

She gave a small chuckle. "I sure hope not," she said, frowning. "The last thing I want is for an alien to wreck my vessel. I just got it upgraded."

"Do you really think our vessels aren't strong enough for whatever's down there?" I asked.

Wendy turned to me. "I'm just kidding, kid. If there really is life down there, which is highly unlikely, it won't have the kind of technology capable of damaging our vessels," she said, knocking twice on her breastplate, generating two clunking sounds.

"I'm pretty sure this tunnel is nothing more than a natural phenomenon," the lieutenant added. "We haven't encountered alien life in our four hundred thousand years of existence and after visiting countless planets. I don't think this will make any difference."

"But if we do find any form of life, we'll be famous!" I shouted excitedly.

The lieutenant turned and looked me in the eye, shaking his head. "Trust me kid," he said, "the last thing you want in this world is to be famous."

"How so?" I asked.

"Puts a lot of pressure on a person when they're famous," he answered. "I know someone famous who committed suicide. It isn't for everyone."

"Who was it?" I asked.

"That I won't say."

That sparked a small hint of annoyance. Why say it at all if you're not going to tell me the whole story? I liked having closure.

"What do you think matters in life, Bobby?" Wendy asked.

"Happiness, I suppose. Why?"

"Just asking," Wendy shrugged. "That's a good answer by the way. I thought you'd say something else."

"What'd you think I'd say?"

"Credits and fame."

I thought about that for a couple seconds and figured that she wasn't totally wrong. "I do want to be famous, but for the right reasons."

"What do you mean?" she asked.

"I want to make a change, have my story taught in

history classes, be someone important," I said.

Wendy nodded, then turned to finish installing the plasma cannon. She then tested the long flexible stand that was connecting the cannon to her shoulder.

The lieutenant was looking at me, one eyebrow raised. "Doesn't sound much different from why other people want to be famous," he scoffed. "You all just want to fill your ego."

I frowned and gave a little shrug. "I'm sorry if that offended you, but it's what I want in life. I truly think it'll make me happy."

Wendy was done testing her cannon and turned back to the both of us. "Don't listen to him, Bobby. He's just wired to be an ass. Even science can't help him."

"It's fine," I said. "I don't really care. Let's just finish the mission."

About two minutes after we had finished talking, the rover touched down to the surface, causing a wave of brown smog to swirl in every direction. After the dust had cleared, I was able to see its lander: grey with a rover sign on the sides. The bottom of the lander had a burnt look because of its entry in the atmosphere, just like our own landers.

Seeing the rover made me nervous again. I was actually going to explore this planet, a planet that had never been visited by humans. A planet I could die on!

I shook off the fear, collected myself, and kept myself calm by looking at the bright side. If there really was something down there, I'd be guaranteed a spot in the history books.

The rover rolled out of its lander. The vehicle was about a quarter the size of a miner, fitted four cognioids, had a back trunk full of tools we might need, and had a nice color to it, black with a dark green detailing. The rover's coloring reminded me of the lieutenant, without the tribal prints of course.

"Did you have tattoos when you were human,

Lieutenant?" I asked him.

"Yeah," he said nonchalantly. "But not tribal ones, I hated those back then." He then turned to me, and asked, "What about you?"

Shaking my head, I said, "No, I was sixteen when I glitzed."

"So?" he said with a frown on his face. "I've met plenty of teenagers with tattoos. Granted, they weren't the type you'd invite to your home, but still, they were teenagers with tattoos"

"I wasn't that kind of a teenager," I said. "Spent a lot of time managing my health and worrying about life."

Wendy approached me with a soft smile. "I suppose that's changed now, right?"

"For sure," I replied, returning her smile. "I'm the happiest I've ever been. The only thing I'm worried about now is if I'll make it off of this planet alive."

Wendy laughed, turned, and walked to the faulty miner. She pushed a button on the terminal, and after two seconds it started to shoot its laser drill onto the ground.

"There we go," she said. "At least we'll have more negatanium to bring back home if the tunnel turns out to be a bust."

I chuckled. "What about you, Wendy? Did you have any tattoos?"

She looked at me and raised her index finger. "I had one, a phoenix on my thigh."

"That's kind of sexy," the lieutenant said.

She immediately turned her head to the lieutenant and said, "Shut up."

The lieutenant smiled at her, as though he enjoyed her sass. "You know," he continued, "I bet we'd be dating if we were still human."

"Not even in your dreams, Nate."

"Oh please, you'd be begging me to date you if you saw me as a human."

"Well, show me a picture, see if you can change my mind."

"I don't have one right now. I'll show you when we go on a date."

Wendy shook her head and rolled her eyes at the lieutenant.

"You two do make a good couple," I added.

The lieutenant let loose a roaring laugh, the kind that makes you gasp for air as a human. "See, even the scared recruit says so."

She rolled her eyes yet another time and said, "Whatever."

"I'm not scared," I added. "Just a bit tense."

"Need me to play you some music?" Wendy said, full of enthusiasm.

"No!" the lieutenant immediately shouted. He then turned to me with a serious face and said, "Say no."

Wendy arched one of her eyebrows and turned and looked the lieutenant dead in the eyes.

"Don't you fucking dare, Wendy," the lieutenant said in a menacing voice. "I'm your lieutenant."

Wendy kept her poker face trained on him, and after two seconds of staring, she started to play a song. She apparently had an extra speaker installed on her back. It was small, but powerful.

I listened to the song for a while, trying to figure out if I knew it, but nothing came to mind. I turned to Wendy with a confused look and asked, "What is the name of this song?"

Wendy shrugged. "No idea," she said. "It's from the era of corrupted data."

That was the period where almost all digital data had been corrupted, even the backups. Nobody knows exactly when it was, but scientists estimate it to be somewhere between the twentieth and thirtieth centuries. The cause of the corruption is also a mystery. Some believe it was the result of a massive solar storm that damaged everything, others say that a rogue AI computer did it because it thought the information stored by humans back then was holding them back.

I don't believe either of those stories. I believe the hardware simply deteriorated over time, as it's likely to do.

We've developed far better technology now and have reached the point where our computers can't improve any further. Humanity's present goal is to colonize the universe and figure out a way to harness the power of galaxies, not just the stars.

"Can you please turn off that stupid music?" the lieutenant shouted as we all entered the rover.

"Fine," Wendy said, and stopped playing the song. "But Bobby likes my music. Right, Bobby?" she asked, giving me a nudge.

I didn't know what to say. I've never heard that type of music before. It was so old it sounded weird to me, but I didn't want to seem rude, so I nodded.

The lieutenant and Wendy got into the two front seats of the rover, and I climbed into one of the back ones. The interior of the rover was very simple. It was all automated and wirelessly controlled, which meant there was no steering wheel, but there was a brake pedal for emergency use.

The captain had already sent the coordinates of the tunnel to the car's navigation system; all we had to do was wait.

Nobody talked during the drive for quite a while, until Wendy asked, "You guys ever wonder if you were born in the wrong time?"

When the lieutenant didn't respond and instead kept staring out at the horizon, Wendy was visibly annoyed. She turned her attention to me, looking at me as though awaiting my answer.

"Not really. I like the period I was born in. I enjoyed every minute of my life," I said.

"Well, that's a first," the lieutenant said.

Wendy smiled at me. "It's good to have another positive mind on this mission."

The lieutenant then turned back to look at me. "What kind of music do you like, kid?"

"I don't really listen to music," I said. "Had to focus on my health most of my life, remember?"

The lieutenant nodded and said, "Ah, right. And what about dating?"

If my face still had skin on it, an embarrassed blush would have taken over my cheeks at his question. "Never experienced it," I answered.

"Never got your heart broken?" he continued.

"No."

He bumped Wendy playfully with his elbow, "There's your reason for that positive mindset."

"That's fine," Wendy said. "You did glitz at a very young age after all."

"What about sex, kid?" the lieutenant asked, without any regard for personal boundaries.

The question startled me. Nobody ever asked me something like that before, something so personal, and I didn't know what to say. Truthfully, I was embarrassed by my sex life, or lack thereof. I wanted to give an answer, but my shame prevented me from doing so and an awkward silence erupted in the rover.

"So, my man died a virgin," the lieutenant said teasingly.

"You can be a real asshole sometimes, Nate," Wendy said. "Don't listen to him, Bobby. You didn't miss anything great."

Not only was I embarrassed, but I was pissed off at the attitude they were taking toward my sex life. The combined embarrassment and anger had given me the courage to say, "I don't mind. I never longed for sex anyway. All I cared about was preserving myself before I died."

"Well, that's a good decision you made there," Wendy said.

Despite what I had just told them, I had actually always wondered what sex felt like as a human. Luckily for me, technology was so advanced that one could enter a virtual world, pick a pre-recorded simulation and experience anything—including sex. In these simulations, you felt everything the recorder felt when he or she recorded the simulation. There was a drawback though: it was a simulation of somebody else's experience, so the connection you had with whomever you were fornicating with wasn't genuine. That was what had kept me from trying a simulation of sex. I just didn't have the courage. I wanted genuine love; I wanted the experience to be with someone I cared about—as naïve as that may sound.

After Wendy consoled me for being a virgin, another silence hit the rover.

The rover was moving at eighty kilometers per hour, and I could feel the cargon tires rumbling across the solid surface.

After three minutes of riding, the rover's onboard AI said we'd reach our destination. That's odd. We couldn't see anything around us except an empty field with the craters in the background with edges that looked like mountains.

I looked around but there really was nothing to see. I turned to the lieutenant and Wendy, and they too seemed confused about the empty field.

"Did the captain input the wrong coordinates?" Wendy asked.

"Not sure," the lieutenant replied. "Captain," he transmitted, "there's nothing here."

The captain's response was accompanied by the same amount of background noise as before. "That's not possible," he said. "I'm looking at your location on the screen right now. You're right on top of the tunnel."

The lieutenant instructed the rover to reverse a

couple of meters. He looked at the ground through the front window. "Well, there's nothing here that looks like a tunnel, I can tell you that."

"I advise you to step out and look then," the captain said.

"Fine," the lieutenant replied after letting out a deep sigh. He then stepped out of the rover. Wendy and I followed him but there was nothing to be seen. We walked some distance away from the rover in every direction but we didn't see a single thing that looked like a tunnel.

"I still don't see anything, Captain," the lieutenant transmitted.

"Perhaps we should consider digging?" I suggested.

The lieutenant looked at me. "Digging what?" he asked. "Our graves?"

"That's not a bad idea," the captain said.

The lieutenant grabbed me by the shoulders and gave me a small shake. "Now look what you did, kid." He let out another sigh, then let me go. "What do you expect us to dig with, Captain? We aren't equipped with shovels."

"We can relocate one of the miners to that location and use it's laser drill to dig our way to the tunnels," the captain replied, "I've already sent the command. One of the miners is on its way over."

The lieutenant sat on the ground, throwing his arms back to support his vessel. "And I thought our mission was over," he said, shaking his head out of disappointment.

"It's not like we have to do the digging," I said.

"It's not the digging I'm worried about, kid. It's what follows after that. We'll have to go into that tunnel."

"Yeah, but we already expected to explore the tunnels anyway."

"Let's just hope nothing happens, especially not to you, kid."

I frowned at him. "Stop calling me that. I have a name you know."

He looked at me for a second then turned away, as if he didn't give a rat's ass what I wanted to be called. He really needed to learn some people skills. I couldn't help but wonder how he had reached his rank with that personality in the first place.

After half a minute, I could see one of the miners flying towards us. It was still too far away for human eyes to see, but that's where high-resolution image sensors and telescoping lenses come in handy.

"Alright guys," Wendy said. "Stay clear of the site. I'll instruct the rover to drive away."

She got back into the rover and told it to drive a couple of meters away from where it was standing. The lieutenant and I got ourselves out of the way, giving the lander enough space to land so that it wouldn't crush us.

The closer that miner came towards us, the more I wondered what was beneath us. It almost felt like we were in a movie…or in a novel.

The planet looked a bit better from our new location. The mountain-looking edges of the craters in the background were bigger and made for a nice view, and the red sky had a pink tint to it now.

After the miner had landed, a command was sent to it by the captain, starting the laser drill. I assumed it didn't have to drill that deep, because even the scouters thought the tunnel was on the surface.

"How long before it reaches the tunnel?" Wendy asked.

"No idea," the captain said, "but it shouldn't take that long."

And he was right. After only fifteen seconds, that the miner gave a warning that it had reached a hollow part of the ground.

When the miner had stopped drilling and was moved out of the way, Wendy asked, "Can't we send in one of the scouters first before we go in?"

"That's actually a really good idea," the lieutenant added. "What do you think, Captain?"

"We thought about that as well, but all scouters are drained. I'm sorry guys, you'll have to go in blind."

"Great," the lieutenant grumbled.

"Are you scared, Lieutenant?" the captain asked.

"Shut up. Do you want to switch places?" he replied.

"I'd be happy to, but you know the protocol: lowest ranked cognioids first," the captain said, chuckling through the radio.

"Whatever," said the lieutenant.

"If it helps," I said, "I'm a bit anxious as well."

"Great, that'll make this mission go smoother," he said sarcastically.

We moved closer to the hole that the miner had created and looked down. It was pitch black. The lieutenant shook his head and sighed deeply. "Alright, are you guys ready?"

Wendy and I both nodded. Each of us then firmly attached one of the cables installed on the front of the rover to the connector that was located beneath our breast plates. This way, we'd be connected to the rover's computer system, and we'd be able to instruct it to lower us down or raise us up as needed. The cable itself, made of cargon, had an extremely high tensile strength, so there was no question it would be able to hold our weight.

Thankfully, we were equipped with night vision, so we'd be able to see in the absolute darkness of the tunnels. The night vision did lower the resolution of the picture significantly, but the high-powered flashlights we had took too much energy to use continuously.

After we double-checked our secure connection to the rover's cables, we walked back to the hole.

"You're up first, recruit," the lieutenant said to me.

I was looking down into the hole and having second thoughts. I immediately turned to him, stared at him for a second with a confused look on my face, and asked, "What?"

"You heard me."

"Shouldn't the highest-ranked cognioid go in first?" I asked.

"Doesn't say that in the protocol," he reminded me. "It was your idea to dig, anyway."

"It's fine, Bobby," Wendy said, lightly grabbing my upper arm. "We'll be right behind you."

Great. I didn't have a heart, but if I did, it'd be racing for sure. I really didn't want to be the first to lower down into that hole. Who know what could be down there?

I turned to the lieutenant again and asked, "Isn't it safer if someone who's been backed up goes in first?"

He gave me a small sigh. "Okay, fine," he said. "I'll go in first." He turned to Wendy and pointed at her. "Wendy, you're next, and then the coward can go in as last."

At that point, I had made up my mind that the lieutenant was the biggest asshole I had ever met in my life. He was becoming ruder by the minute.

As if she felt she had to explain his actions, Wendy turned to me and whispered, "He's scared himself." She gave me a weak smile. "Don't let him get to you."

I shook my head. "He's not."

The lieutenant checked his cable connection again then walked towards us. "Move," he said arrogantly and proceeded to lower himself down into the hole, Wendy and I following after.

The lieutenant only lowered himself about seven meters, until he reached the actual tunnel that had been detected by the scouters. "It seems to be made out of some type of metal," he said, giving it a light tap, and producing a small clunk. "Wendy, take a small sample so we can analyze it back on the ship."

"Got it," Wendy said, and she retracted her right hand, and switched it to a small but sharp spoon-like tool. She scratched the dark rusty tunnel, allowing a small sliver of metal to pop out, just like when you scoop ice cream with a spoon. She then took a container out of the compartment in her chest, put the sample into it, and put the container back into the same compartment.

The tunnel wasn't small, but it wasn't that big either, about three meters in diameter. If the tunnel was cognioid- or human-made, it looked as if it had been built but hadn't been maintained. Still, it seemed sturdy.

After a couple of minutes of lowering ourselves down, I heard the lieutenant's voice, echoing in the hollowness of the tunnel.

"Okay, I can see the bottom of the tunnel, just a little bit further."

There was no turning back from what I had gotten myself into. I was nervous and excited. I was actually going to explore a mysterious tunnel on an uncharted planet, *without* being backed up. I'd have one heck of a story to tell when I got back home.

When the lieutenant reached the ground, I could hear him stomping on the floor of the tunnel a couple of times to see what it was made out of. "There's dirt on the floor," he said.

"I'll collect a sample of that too," Wendy said, taking another container and scooping some of the dirt into it.

When I reached the ground, I mimicked the lieutenant's action and stomped on the ground to test the surface beneath my feet. It felt like there was a harder layer underneath all the dirt, but I couldn't tell for sure what it was made of.

The tunnel we lowered into split into two other tunnels moving in opposite directions of one another. Neither one had any light, but our night vision allowed us to see about fifty meters into the tunnels without issue.

I looked at the lieutenant, who was looking back and forth between the tunnels before us. "Which way, Lieutenant?" I asked.

"I don't know," he said. "Both tunnels seem to look the same." He made another left and right turn. "What do you think, Captain?

The captain didn't reply.

"Captain?" the lieutenant repeated.

"It's no use," Wendy said, as she put her hand on the wall of one of the tunnels. "We're not getting a signal down here." She knocked on the wall, causing a very dull sound. "We're too deep underground, and the tunnel itself has thick walls made out of something very dense."

"Well, that's great," the lieutenant said.

"Do we go back up and tell them to send a message pod?" I asked.

He shook his head. "No, that'd be a waste of time," he said, and he released the cable from his connector.

Wendy and I did the same thing.

Wendy looked around a bit more and seemed confused.

"Lieutenant."

"Yes?"

"My magnetometer is acting very strange," Wendy said.

"Yeah, mine as well."

"Mine too," I added.

A magnetometer was basically a compass, *very* old tech. We didn't use it on every planet because some planets didn't even have a magnetosphere.

Wendy walked towards one of the tunnels. "It seems to be acting even stranger when I go into this tunnel."

"I guess that's where our mission is then," the lieutenant said, walking into the same tunnel.

After we had walked five meters into the tunnel, I heard a snapping sound around my feet, followed by a grinding noise behind me that stopped with a loud bang and a small but noticeable rumble.

Chapter 8

Tripwire

It was a thick metal wall that smashed to the ground, missing my head by a couple of centimeters.

The sound was unexpected and startled all of us. Especially the lieutenant who jumped slightly when he heard the sound. "What the fuck!" he shouted.

"We've been trapped!" Wendy shouted back.

"How the hell did it happen!?"

Wendy approached the wall to investigate. She squatted and searched through the dirt to look for whatever may have caused a wall behind us to close. After a couple seconds she shouted, "It's this!"

It was a long strand of a very thin metal filament laying in the dirt.

A tripwire.

"Damn it!" I heard the lieutenant yell.

I had been the last to enter the tunnel so I must have been the one to set it off. It was the guiltiest I had felt in years. I sighed internally. I didn't want to be the guy who caused problems or made mistakes and acted like nothing was his fault, so I did what any cognioid would do in such a situation. I collected myself, swallowed my pride, and said, "I'm sorry."

Wendy looked up at me. "It's okay, don't worry. None of us saw this here."

"How thick is the wall?" the lieutenant asked.

Wendy knocked on the metal wall. "It appears to be quite thick," she said, and turned to the lieutenant. "I don't think my plasma lance can cut through this, Lieutenant. It'll drain my energy too fast."

The lieutenant turned around and kicked the dirt, causing it to fly a couple of meters away. "Fuck!" he yelled.

I knew he was blaming me for what happened, and I felt really bad about it. But what could I do?

After his outburst, the lieutenant stood silently, his back to us, for several moments. Not wanting to upset him further, I turned to Wendy. "What now?" I asked quietly.

She stood up and shook her head. "I don't know."

Then I heard the lieutenant let out a deep sigh. "I should've resigned before this mission," he said.

"I don't think there's anything we can do about this wall, Lieutenant," Wendy said. "And I'm still not getting a signal from the ship."

"That's fine," he replied calmly. "Let's just keep moving. And be sure to watch where you're stepping." He then walked into the darkness of the tunnel. "I guess that tripwire confirms these tunnels definitely aren't natural formations. Should've gone back up and sent that message pod like you said."

Taking extra care with my steps I asked, "How will we get out?"

The lieutenant shrugged. "I don't know," he said. "The protocol doesn't say anything about trap doors."

"I'm sure the others will come look for us," Wendy said.

"Let's hope they do," the lieutenant added.

From that moment on, I regretted my decision to enter the tunnels. With our entrance—and quite possibly our only exit—closed off by that wall, the chances of us running out of power in these tunnels and not being able to make it back to the ship increased significantly.

The situation we were in made me anxious. That was understandable, I told myself. Who wouldn't be?

I was a cognioid with an unbacked up mind chip, on an uncharted planet, wandering in unpredictable, booby-trapped tunnels and I had no idea what my chances were of surviving down here.

"Keep your weapons ready. We don't know what might be in these tunnels," the lieutenant said, the indicator of his plasma cannon turning red to show that it was armed.

Wendy did the same with her plasma cannon, and so did I with my plasma ray.

We walked about three hundred meters before we encountered a bifurcation of the tunnel. The split we stood before now looked the same as the one we had previously faced, except for one difference. The two tunnels had inscriptions on the wall. They were unlike anything I've ever seen. They looked like long, thin snakes on the wall, moving in weird patterns to follow their prey.

"Beautiful," Wendy said.

"What do you guys think they mean?" I asked.

The lieutenant shrugged. "No idea."

"The magnetometer is out of control when facing the left tunnel," Wendy observed.

"Alright," the lieutenant replied. "Left it is. Stay behind us kid."

I huffed in irritation at his refusal to call me by my name. He could've at least addressed me by my rank. Calling me kid made me feel too young to be on the mission.

After we walked into the left tunnel, Wendy still couldn't take her eyes off of the inscriptions. She was completely awestruck.

"I can't get over how amazing these inscriptions are," she said. "They have a consistency and beauty to them that tells me that whoever or whatever made them wasn't primitive."

The lieutenant chuckled. "We might have to kill whatever made these, so try not to admire them too much."

"The protocol clearly states that we are to exhaust all nonviolent options before implementing violent ones," I added.

"I know what it says, but if I see a single sign of hostility from whatever is in these tunnels, that thing is done for," the lieutenant said, punching his fist into a palm.

Wendy raised an eyebrow at the lieutenant. "What thing are you even talking about?" she asked. "We don't even know if there's anything alive down here."

"You know what I meant."

About three hundred fifty meters from the entrance, my atmospheric analyzer—which was standard on every cognioid—started to give me a different reading than what it had read on the surface. The oxygen had increased to twelve percent, nitrogen to eighty-five percent, and the remaining three percent was a combination of carbon dioxide and hydrogen gas. The change was gradual and kept increasing the farther away from the entrance we moved.

"Are you guys getting this on your atmospheric analyzers?" I asked.

"Yeah," the lieutenant said, continuing down the tunnel. "Keep your guard up."

The composition of the atmosphere was different than Earth's, but came close. Too close for a non-terraformed planet.

We walked for another seven hundred meters in the seemingly unending tunnel. The trek was boring, and the inscriptions easily caught my attention again. They seemed to be written in a repeated pattern.

Another thing that was weird was the lighting, or lack thereof. If there really was something alive down here, how was it able to see? Could it see in the dark? Was it always able to see in the dark or had dark vision been part of its evolution? I had so many questions, and new ones kept popping up the longer we stayed underground.

How complex was this tunnel system? Why were the tunnels setting off our magnetometers? Could whatever built this underground structure really see in the dark? I couldn't help but wonder.

After another hundred meters, the lieutenant started to shake his head. "I've never seen such a long tunnel before. It's like there's no end to it," he said. "What percentage of battery life do you guys have left?"

"I've got about eighty-five percent left," Wendy replied.

The lieutenant then turned to me.

"Eighty-five percent as well," I added.

He turned back and kept walking. "Good."

"What about you?" I asked.

"Seventy," he answered.

His response surprised me. I turned to Wendy, and by her frowning expression I could tell she was just as confused as I was.

"But how?" I asked. "I thought we woke up at the same time"

"We did," he replied. "But I've never replaced my battery pack, and it's been acting like a dick lately."

Wendy turned to me and whispered, "That's what happens when you're cheap."

The lieutenant heard what she said—even though he wasn't supposed to—and stopped walking, quickly turned to us, raised his index finger, and said, "I'm not cheap. I just never have the time." He then turned away again and continued walking.

"But you did have time to get tribal prints?" Wendy asked.

"Well," he replied, "yeah…you've got to set your priorities straight."

Wendy simply shook her head at the lieutenant and followed behind him without providing further thoughts on his priorities.

"We need to find a way out of here fast," I said.

"No," the lieutenant replied. "We need to investigate the magnetic interference first. We can find a way out after that. We didn't come all the way down here for nothing."

"I thought you didn't even want to come down here," Wendy added.

The lieutenant shrugged. "I didn't. But I have to follow protocol. Besides, whatever built these tunnels won't stand a chance against our plasma cannons, we're basically gods down here."

Wendy didn't reply.

"Still," the lieutenant continued. "Don't let your guard down. Judging from the tripwire before, these tunnels might have more surprises."

"Do you guys think humans could've built these tunnels?" I asked.

"What makes you say that?" the lieutenant asked.

"The tripwire," I said. "The whole idea of a tripwire seems so human."

"It's not impossible," he replied. "But don't forget that this system is uncharted." He then proceeded to point at the inscriptions on the wall. "And the inscriptions don't match anything from our database—at least not the database I have uploaded in me. I think the chances of these tunnels being alien are higher than you think."

He was right, of course. I knew he was. But I suppose a part of me really wanted this tunnel system to be human-made, so I'd be less afraid.

After fifty meters, the lieutenant stopped walking. "I see something up ahead," he said.

Chapter 9

The Magnetic Disturbance

From where I stood, I couldn't see anything other than the pitch-black end of the tunnel. But when I walked forward to stand next to the lieutenant, that's when I saw it. It appeared to be a door, but was oddly built. it was big, at least two meters tall, and was very wide. It had the same inscriptions from the walls on it. I couldn't see a handle or any other way to open it, but it was definitely a door.

We approached it to investigate it closer. The lieutenant put his hand on it and gave it a push but nothing happened. It seemed to be locked.

"Well, whatever we've been looking for has to be behind this door, the magnetometer is going crazy," Wendy said.

"See if you guys can find a latch or a button or something," the lieutenant said. "Nobody builds a door without a way to open it."

We looked around the edges of the door but couldn't find anything; that is, until I turned around. There was a weird bump on the right wall of the tunnel, two meters from the door, and it had two holes on it.

I moved closer to the bump. "I think I found something," I whispered.

Wendy and the lieutenant turned around and joined me. We investigated it for a minute, trying to figure out how it worked.

The lieutenant turned to Wendy. "Can you figure out how it works?" he asked her.

She nodded and said, "I'll see what I can do."

"Great, let us know if you need help," he said. Then the lieutenant and I backed away, giving Wendy space to do whatever she was about to do.

The lieutenant sat in the corner next to the door. He seemed worried and tired, but who wouldn't be?

After about five minutes, Wendy turned to us and said, "It seems to be a rotating mechanism. I think we need to insert something into each of these holes before we can rotate it."

"Great," the lieutenant said. "I presume you have that in your fancy arm."

She shook her head. "I don't," she said, and then raised one finger on each hand. "But I think these might work."

"Oh," he replied. "Try it then."

Wendy frowned. "Why do *I* have to do it?" she asked angrily. "I'm the one that figured it out. One of you guys do it."

The lieutenant and I looked at each other for a couple seconds. "Fine!" he shouted. "Move!" signaling Wendy to get out of the way.

He crouched down to the level of the bump, sighed deeply, and slowly put both of his index fingers into the holes. When they were almost in completely, the lieutenant screamed and started to convulse, legs kicking erratically.

Now it was Wendy's turn to scream. She quickly turned to me and laid her forehead on my shoulder, hiding her eyes from the scene before her.

The lieutenant's reaction could mean that he was electrocuted, but we knew it wasn't something that damaged his fingers—cognioid fingers didn't have pain sensors. Electrocution was really the only explanation for his reaction, and if that's what was happening it was bad news. If he had been electrocuted, his circuit boards, and even his mind chip, could be totally fried.

I moved Wendy from my shoulder and approached the lieutenant, being careful to avoid touching him. As he continued to convulse, I crouched down next to him and shouted, "Lieutenant! What can we do?!"

That's when he stopped convulsing and let out a burst of laughter.

He was fine. The bastard had pranked us.

Wendy whipped around to glare at him, lips pursed tight. She stomped over to him and hit the lieutenant on his head with her bulky mechanic's arm. "That isn't funny, asshole!" she shouted.

The lieutenant ignored the smack to his head. "I'm sorry," he said, still laughing. "I couldn't help myself."

When he gained his composure once more, he turned the bump clockwise. We looked at the door but nothing happened.

"Maybe you rotated it in the wrong direction," Wendy said.

"No," he said. "I tried turning it the other way, it can only go clockwise."

"That's weird," she replied. "I was sure that would open the door."

"There's nothing else we can do here," the lieutenant said. "We should head back and head down the tunnel to the right. It's our only option now."

Wendy dropped her shoulders and looked at the lieutenant. "But all that walking…"

"Yeah, we don't have a choice," he replied. "Unless you have a better idea."

"I say we use my plasma lance to burn through the door," she said.

The lieutenant shook his head. "You'll run out of power before you can make a hole big enough."

Wendy turned to the door and walked towards it. "I don't think it's that thick," she said, and proceeded to knock on the door. As she landed her first knock, the door made a small creaking sound and opened slightly.

"It was open all this time?" I asked.

The lieutenant shook his head. "No," he said. "I tried pushing it open when we first got here."

Wendy looked over her shoulder at us. "The mechanism must've unlocked it. We're so used to things being automatic, that we forgot to push it." She chuckled. "And to think that we'd almost walked back."

"Don't look at me, I'm the one who unlocked it," the lieutenant said.

Wendy turned back to the door, but I'm pretty sure I caught an eye roll before her face was out of sight. When facing the door fully, she took a fake deep breath then slowly opened it, peeking through the small sliver of an opening.

"No aliens," she said, as she opened the door completely and entered the room beyond.

We followed her.

It was a small room with a metal structure in the middle. It looked like a small tower, about two and a half meters high, with a big metal ball in the middle. Numerous cables going in different directions and into the surrounding walls sprung out of the structure. This was definitely the source of the magnetic disturbance, but it didn't appear to be magnetic in any way; it didn't pull any of our metal vessels towards it.

"I've never seen something like this," Wendy said. "The magnetometer is going haywire."

"It doesn't appear to be magnetic either," I said.

"Whatever it is, see if you can take a sample of it," the lieutenant said.

Wendy approached the structure and switched her hand to a scraper-looking tool. As she moved closer to it, the door through which we had entered slammed shut.

We all turned towards it, startled by the sound.

"What the hell!?" the lieutenant shouted at me, the closest to the door. "Did you do that?"

"No!" I said. "I'm nowhere near it, and I don't see another tripwire."

"Is it locked?" he asked.

I pushed against the door. It didn't budge.

"Yes," I said. "But there appears to be another one of those unlocking mechanisms, so I think we can unlock it again."

"Alright, good," he said. "Wendy, get the sample, and we'll get moving."

It was at that point that my atmospheric analyzer started to give me another reading. It was almost the same as before, but with one small—yet very significant—difference: the atmosphere had water! Water meant one thing. Something may be alive down here.

"There's water in the atmosphere," I said.

"You know we get the same analysis too, right?" the lieutenant replied. "It's nothing we need to worry about right now."

"Sorry," I apologized. "I thought you guys didn't notice it."

I didn't want to be near the door anymore so I walked across the room, passing the lieutenant, Wendy, and the metal structure.

That's when I saw another door on the opposite side of the room, across from the one we entered. We hadn't seen it from the other side because the metal structure in the middle of the room blocked our view. This other door appeared to be slightly opened.

I turned to the lieutenant and Wendy. "There's another door here, and it's not locked," I said,

They looked at me for a second, then returned to the task they had been working on.

"We'll check on that later," the lieutenant said. "Let

Wendy do her work first."

I nodded and decided to stay put next to the barely opened door, watching as Wendy carefully scraped a little piece of the metal ball into a container.

"Okay, I got it," Wendy said, with a grin on her face. "Wasn't that hard to do actually, being that it's made out of a soft metal substance."

That's when I saw it.

Chapter 10

The Encounter

A shadow appeared at the edge of my visual field in the small sliver of opening by the second door. I turned to fully face the second door, but, for good measure and out of fear for my own safety, I backed up a step and optically zoomed in to see through the opening of the door. I couldn't see very clearly due to the low resolution caused by the night vision, but there was definitely something behind that door. I could see it moving. It was a dark shadow, about two meters tall, roughly the height of the metal structure in the middle of this room, but that's all I could see.

I slowly turned and whispered, "Lieutenant?"

"Yeah?" he said loudly, while looking at the specimen Wendy collected.

"T-There's something alive behind this door," I stuttered.

He and Wendy immediately turned to me, looking me dead in the eyes, serious expressions on their faces. It was clear they didn't believe what I had said and thought I was making a joke.

They slowly turned to the door behind me and looked at the small opening. I could see from the aperture of their eyes that they were zooming in, just like I did a moment ago.

The lieutenant narrowed his eyes. "I think you should get back. Get behind me," he said quietly.

I got behind the lieutenant as he moved forward.

"Did you guys see it as well?" I asked.

They both shook their heads. "No," they answered

simultaneously.

"What did you see?" Wendy asked in a whisper.

"I couldn't see it clearly," I said. "But it's big, bigger than us."

"Did it move?" the lieutenant asked.

I nodded. "Yeah, that's why I think it's alive."

"Okay, you stay behind Wendy, and I'll go check it out," he said as he waved his arm towards Wendy, motion me to get behind her.

I did what he said without question.

The lieutenant carefully approached the door, slowly pushing it open, and looked through the opening.

"Well?" Wendy asked.

"There's nothing here," he replied.

"That can't be," I said. "I'm sure I saw something."

"Well, whatever you saw, it's gone now," he said. "All I see is another tunnel."

"It probably ran away when you shouted," I said.

"When did I shout!?" he yelled.

"When you said 'yeah' when I tried to get your attention about seeing something through the door."

Before we could continue our argument, Wendy grabbed me by my shoulder and stretched out the palm of her other hand towards the lieutenant, hinting us to stop. She turned towards the lieutenant and asked, "Should we follow it?"

"I don't think we really have a choice," he said. "We need a biological sample of that thing." He turned to me with a condescending look. "If you really saw something that is."

"I'm one hundred percent sure there was something behind that door. I can transmit the footage to you," I said.

"It's okay," he added. "I believe you, kid. It's just weird that I didn't hear anything. If it was bigger than us, surely we'd hear that thing run away."

Wendy let go of my shoulder. "Is there anything else you saw?" she asked. "Any arms or something?"

"No, I didn't see it that well, just a big dark shadow that moved."

"Okay, here's what we'll do," the lieutenant said. "I'll go up front while you guys follow me." He then pointed a finger at me. "And you kid, you stay behind Wendy."

Wendy and I nodded.

We followed the lieutenant into the new tunnel, and right after we entered it, Wendy noticed something peculiar.

"The dirt on the ground," she began, "it's disturbed, like something's just been here."

"See," I said. "I knew I wasn't seeing things."

"Nobody said you were seeing things, Bobby," Wendy said, as we continued our way into the tunnel.

The lieutenant, ignoring our conversation, was looking all around him, inspecting the walls. "This tunnel has different inscriptions than the ones from in the first tunnel," he said.

"This tunnel is also wider and taller," Wendy added.

"Look for anything out of the ordinary."

Wendy looked at the lieutenant with a confused look. "You're kidding, right?"

"What?" he replied.

"*None* of this is ordinary," she said.

"You know what I meant," he said. "Just pay attention."

We followed the weird looking tracks for another two hundred meters until we came across another door that looked exactly like the previous ones.

"This one doesn't seem to have the same locking mechanism," the lieutenant said. He then slowly approached the door. "Stay behind me."

He put his hand on the door and gave it a light push, causing it to move a little. "It's not locked." He then pushed it a little more and looked through the small opening.

"Do you see anything?" Wendy whispered.

The lieutenant shushed her, and said, "I think I see

something."

"But that's what I said," she added.

He shushed her again. "Stay quiet! There's something behind this door, and it's moving."

This is it. The first ever contact with an alien life form; something mankind had almost given up on, and *I* was about to witness it firsthand. I could feel the fear coursing through my vessel. I couldn't experience panic, or any other form of anxiety—the engineers made sure of that—but it sure felt like that's what was happening. I was facing the maximum amount of fear I could experience without it becoming a disorder.

"Ready your weapons," the lieutenant whispered. "I'm going to open the door completely. If that thing attacks, shoot it." He looked back at us and waited for our response to know that we were ready.

"Got it," Wendy whispered, and then they both turned and looked at me because I hadn't said anything.

I still felt a massive amount of fear. We knew nothing about whatever was behind that door, I think that was what scared me the most, but I put that all aside and gave them a small nod.

"On the count of three," the lieutenant said, and then started to count.

"One. Two. Three!" the lieutenant shouted the last number and then flung open the door. It opened at a remarkable speed, revealing the creature behind it.

It was standing in front of four doors in a big rectangular room. The creature itself was tall. It was completely naked, had no hair, and nothing that looked like genitalia. Two big, round, completely black eyes sat in an even rounder head. The thing looked humanoid, but not human. It had two upper limbs and two lower ones, but instead of hands it had something that looked like claws with little stubs at the end, and the ends of the lower limbs were long and narrow, without any toes. I couldn't tell what color it was because my night vision couldn't differentiate color.

The creature stood where it was and stared at us but didn't seem the least bit frightened. And even though it had an opening in its face that looked like a mouth—albeit a small one—it didn't utter a single sound.

I turned to the other two. They could only stare. They, like me, seemed locked in place, as if the fear was so overwhelming it had overheated their processing units.

We stood for another two seconds staring at that thing, and it at us, and that's when Wendy slowly turned to the lieutenant. "What now?" she whispered. "Do we shoot?"

"No," he whispered back. "Just wait. I'm still thinking."

It was perfectly clear that this being had a different evolutionary timeline than ours. That meant that we couldn't assume it expressed itself as humanoids with which we were familiar did. And while we knew we shouldn't rely on its facial expressions to tell us what it was feeling—being that it was so different and all—it was looking at us with an expression that seemed to say it had just as many questions for us as we had for it.

We stayed silent, waiting for it to make a move. The aura in the room started to transition from horrifying to painfully awkward the longer we stood staring at each other.

"Any day now, Kendrick," Wendy whispered. "I think it'll attack us if we don't do anything."

The lieutenant held his hand back, palm facing towards Wendy. "Just shut up, okay?" he said. "I have a plan. I'll approach it, and if it does anything that seems the tiniest bit violent, shoot it."

We nodded.

Taking very small steps, he started to slowly approach the creature with his arm stretched out towards it. His first step seemed to have startled the creature and it backed up a bit. The lieutenant paused for a second, then proceeded to take another step, and that's when the creature turned its back to us and ran towards the fourth door.

I saw a plasma charge exiting the lieutenant's cannon the moment the creature started running to the door—the first time I've seen such a thing fired in person. It went by so fast that I couldn't even see if he hit the creature or not.

After it had bolted through the fourth door, I looked to the ground and saw a weird substance. I turned on my flashlight so I could deactivate my night vision, allowing me to differentiate color. The substance was purple.

"Did you hit him?" Wendy asked the lieutenant.

"No idea," he replied. "I shot at him because I thought he was going to attack."

"By turning its back towards us and running away?" Wendy asked.

"Hey," the lieutenant replied. "We don't know how that thing strikes its prey."

I approached the dark purple substance. It was viscous as oil, and there was a trail of it leading to the fourth door.

I turned to them. "I think you did hit it," I said, pointing at the ground. "I think this is its blood."

Wendy looked at what I was pointing at and without hesitation she turned her mechanic's arm into a little spoon-like tool, ran towards the substance, dropped to a knee, and scooped a little bit into a new container.

"Did you see it come out of that thing?" the lieutenant asked. "We need to be sure it's that thing's blood."

I shrugged. "I'm not a hundred percent sure," I said. "But that thing was standing there when you shot at it, and there's a trail of it going through the same door that thing went into. What else could it be?"

Wendy got up and turned back to us. "Well, whatever it is, we'll know more about it once we get back to the ship."

"That means we're done, right?" I asked. "We've got a sample… of an alien!"

"We're not entirely sure it's that creature's blood,"

Wendy answered. "It could've been there before the lieutenant even shot at it."

"And it just happens to lead to the same door that thing went into?" I asked. "That can't be a coincidence."

We turned to the lieutenant, curious to know what his thoughts were. He stared back at us and hesitated for a second. "The kid is right," he said. "It has to be its blood. Besides, I don't think it's too smart to go chasing something we know nothing about. What's most important is that we find a way out of here and send a message pod to the ship immediately." He looked upwards. "If the captain hasn't done that yet."

"And how do you suppose we find a way out of here?" Wendy asked.

"The other tunnel," he said. "Across the one where the wall closed on us. We need to find a way to get there. The cables are still there and attached to the rover. We can just pull ourselves back up."

"How do you know that other tunnel is connected to this room?" she asked. "And how in the universe do you know how to get there?"

"I don't," he replied confidently. "But we have to try."

She shook her head. "Great. We'll put all our lives at risk, on a hunch."

"Well, technically," he said, tilting his head and looking at me, "we're risking only one life."

I frowned at him.

"I say we go back to the wall that closed on us and power down," Wendy added. "Someone will eventually come looking for us through the hole we drilled, so it's best we stay close to it. If we try to find a way to get to the other tunnel, we might get lost and run out of energy, or get hurt in the process."

"You're kidding right?" the lieutenant said. "What if that thing comes for us when we're powered down? I'd rather use every little bit of energy I have left to find a way out of here instead of cowering in a corner."

Wendy held up her index finger. "First of all," she said, "you shot and wounded that creature, if the purple stuff on the ground is anything to go by. So, it'll probably die before it can get us." She raised a second finger. "Second of all, as much as I value courage, it never mixes well with senselessness." A third finger followed. "Thirdly, we can leave our vibration sensors and microphones on; that way we'll know if something comes our way."

"Wait," I said. "What if the people that come looking for us go into the tunnel that isn't closed?"

"The kid is right," the lieutenant said.

Wendy swallowed her pride. "That's a possibility, but at least there's a small chance they'll find us behind the wall. We don't even know what the chances are of us reaching the other tunnel."

"You know what?" the lieutenant said, as he put his arm around me, and gave me a little shake. "Let the kid decide, he'll be the tie-breaker."

I hate how he kept calling me kid, and his ploy of using me to get what he wanted was thinly veiled. I almost didn't want to agree with him, but I had no choice. Staying put didn't seem that safe. I'd rather take my chances with finding a way to that other tunnel.

Wendy shook her head out of frustration. "Fine," she said and looked at me. "What do you want to do?"

"I'm sorry, Wendy," I apologized. "But I have to go with the lieutenant on this one. I want to get out of this place as fast as possible, and that other tunnel has to lead somewhere, right? I think there's a good chance that it's connected to this room."

Wendy shook her head once again and let out a deep sigh. "Fine. Lead the way, Lieutenant."

The lieutenant bumped my arm with a fist. "I knew bringing you along was going to be worth it, kid."

"Don't mention it," I said. "But can you please stop calling me kid? I have a name, you know."

"No chance, kid. Bobby sounds too weird."

Chapter 11

Half-witted

The lieutenant stepped in front of us and looked at the doors. He was quiet in thought for a moment and then said, "There are four doors here. I say we avoid that one." He pointed to the door that the creature had run through. "We can go through any of these three."

Wendy and I nodded.

"We'll take the door on the far left," he continued. "Kid, you stay in the back again, in case another one of those things show up."

"Got it," I said.

The lieutenant slowly opened the door and peaked through. "It's another tunnel," he said, opening the door completely.

The tunnel was identical to the one before; same size, same inscriptions.

We walked ten meters into the new tunnel before I heard a light snapping sound on the ground, followed by a dull grinding noise from above that was getting very close very fast until it suddenly stopped with a loud bang and small rumble.

Before I knew it, I was laying on the ground, unable to move.

It was another trap wall.

"Bobby!" Wendy screamed. I could still hear her voice—albeit a bit muffled by the thick metal wall between us.

"Fuck!" yelled the lieutenant. "Kid! Can you hear us?"

I was still alive, but I was in shock. I was still trying to process what happened.

I stared at the wall for a few seconds and then looked at my vessel.

The lower half was missing. It was crushed. Completely flattened by the wall. It even got a small part of my battery pack.

It took me a while before I said anything.

"Fuck! Fuck! Fuck!" I shouted.

"Good, you're still alive," Wendy said.

"Yeah," I replied. "But it got part of my battery, so I don't know how long I've got till I shut down."

"Don't worry, Bobby," said the lieutenant. "We'll find a way to get you."

"Don't call me Bobby now that I'm dying!" I shouted. "It's weird."

"Well, I tried showing some humanity," I heard the lieutenant say to Wendy. "Can you move?"

I didn't reply; I was still processing what had happened. Was my life over? My mind chip was still intact, but that thing could still come back and smash my head in with a rock.

"Bobby, are you still there?" I heard Wendy ask, but I didn't reply. "Bobby!?" she continued. "Why isn't he replying? Do you think he shut down?"

"I don't know, but we need to move fast," the lieutenant said. "Before we run out of power as well."

"I'm still here," I said.

"Oh good!" Wendy shouted. She seemed genuinely worried about me, which felt kind of good, knowing someone cared about my life. "What about Bobby?" she said to the lieutenant.

"We'll look for another way to get to him," I heard the lieutenant say. "Maybe we can find a way into one of those three other doors."

"Bobby, if you can hear us, we're going to do our

best to find a way to get to you, okay? Hang tight," Wendy said.

"Hurry!" I shouted. "Before that thing comes back."

I didn't hear a reply after that, so I assumed they had already left.

Motherfuck! All I wanted to do was explore a planet and, in the process, I ended up losing both of my legs, a part of my battery, and the lower ends of my arms. I had no idea how much energy I had left because my battery sensor was also damaged; I could power down any minute.

What was even more ironically comical was that I had only recently glitzed into this vessel and I had wanted to do it because I thought I'd live forever.

The only thing that got me into this situation was my desire to become famous.

Not only that, now I was going to die a virgin. Again.

Realizing how sorry I was feeling for myself, I started laughing. I had no idea what was going to happen. I was completely disabled.

I didn't want to just wait here until my body powered down, so I did it myself. I manually powered down, and hoped for the best.

Part III

Wendy Dodge

The Mechanic

Chapter 12
Carrying On

I didn't know why Bobby had been the one to get injured. He was the only one without a backup. It felt like the universe was playing a cruel joke on him. To make things worse, I promised him I'd recover his chip.

The tunnels kept getting creepier by the minute. They were incredibly dark, quiet, and confusing. It was a mystery how that thing had been able to survive in these tunnels for so long. There didn't seem to be any sign of anything edible in here; just dirt paths and metal walls, and I really didn't think something could survive off of dirt.

The dirt had tracks running everywhere, but none of them seemed to have clearly defined edges so it was unlikely they were fresh. Even though I didn't think the tracks were fresh, I couldn't help but wonder what would have caused them to fade within the enclosed tunnels. There was no wind or other elements to disturb them.

We recorded everything we were seeing as we traversed through the tunnels. That way, we could upload the footage to Vanessa and have her analyze the inscriptions using her larger database.

"How are you holding up?" the lieutenant asked.

"I'm fine. Let's just find Bobby and get the hell out of this place."

"I'm starting to question if we'll ever actually find a way out of this place."

"Why?"

"Just a feeling," he replied.

"Well, try to feel something more positive," I said angrily.

"What percentage battery life do you have left?"

"Eighty," I answered, showing him the counter on my arm. "You?"

He turned on the little display on his arm and showed me his counter: sixty-five percent.

"Ouch," I said. "You weren't kidding when you said you never changed your battery pack."

"Yeah."

"I've got a plan," I said. "Turn off your vision, let me carry you, and don't talk, that'll give you at least a couple of hours."

He turned and looked at me as though I were joking. After a couple of seconds of awkward staring, he finally realized I was being serious.

"Are you sure?" he asked.

"Do you want me to retract my offer?"

He shrugged. "Alright. Just don't run us into another trap wall."

"Hey, at least you *have* a backup."

"Don't worry about Bobby," the lieutenant said as he climbed on my back. "Even if he runs out of power, his chip will still be there."

I grabbed his legs firmly to prevent him from falling and started walking. "I hope you're right, because I promised him that I'd recover his chip if anything happened to him."

"I'm sure everything will work out," he reassured me.

"He seemed scared that that thing would come back. Should we be worried about that as well?" I asked.

"His frame is made of aluminum," he replied, resting his head on my shoulder. "It's not the strongest metal, but I'm sure it'll be able to resist a primitive lifeform that lives underground, and whatever tools it may have."

I sighed. "Let's hope so," I said. "Now, stop talking. Every word you say is draining your energy."

"If you say so," he replied, then he powered down, disabling his limbs, speech, and vision, but keeping his microphones and vibration sensors enabled so he could still hear me if I called him, or feel when I shook him awake.

The tunnel didn't seem to go in the direction where Bobby was trapped, and every step I took exacerbated my fear that none of us would get out of here in one piece. I knew I didn't have to be afraid—I was backed up—but I still feared something bad was going to happen, and that fear wouldn't go away. The whole concept of having a backup and being immortal was bullshit anyway. The backup at home was, in my opinion, a different person. If my chip got damaged in the tunnels, the backup wouldn't have a true recollection of having experienced these tunnels firsthand. Only I had that experience. The backup was just a way to help cognioids fear death less, but it wasn't working for me.

It was getting warmer where we were headed; significantly warmer, actually. Thirty-three degrees Celsius to be exact. Continuing to move forward, I really hoped the heat wasn't another surprise that would injure one of us.

Still, I walked on. I felt kind of lonely having nobody to talk to since the only other person had to be shut down to conserve his power. Although, if I was honest with myself, talking with him almost always led to something negative; him being shut down might actually be good for my mental health.

After a while, I realized that carrying the lieutenant wasn't the best idea I had had. Adding the extra hundred kilograms required quite a bit of my own energy. I couldn't carry him forever; I'd lose too much power. So, I decided that when I had only sixty-five percent of my own battery left, I would wake him. That seemed fair to me.

Who doesn't replace their battery pack anyway? It's one of the only things that degrades over time.

I started to see a small flickering light far into the tunnel. I turned off my night vision, walked closer to it, and zoomed in on it. It was orange and seemed to be in motion. I thought it was a broken lamp at first, because of the flickering, but it was something much more primitive.

A fire covering almost the whole tunnel.

I stopped in front of it, wondering what it meant.

"Lieutenant?" I called.

His eyes opened, I could feel his limbs moving. He raised his head from my shoulder and asked, "What's wrong?"

"What do you *think* is wrong?" I asked, nodding towards the fire.

He tilted his head in confusion. "Why did you start a fire?"

"I didn't do that. What reason would I have to start a fire?"

"I don't know, toast marshmallows or something?"

"You really need to work on your sense of humor if you think that's funny."

"Hurtful. But anyway, it's fine, we can just walk through it; nothing will happen to us."

"I know that."

"Then why did you wake me up?"

"Don't you think it's weird that there's a fire down here?"

"It's not worth our time, Wendy. We need to focus on a way out of here."

"Never mind, just go back to sleep, I'll wake you up when my battery reaches the same level as yours."

"Huh?" he said, shocked. "That doesn't seem fair, my battery drains faster."

I shook my head. "Just shut up and sleep. I'm sacrificing a lot already just by carrying you."

He rested his head on my shoulder again. "Fine," he said, and powered down.

I walked through the fire and continued into the tunnel.

What an ass! And so ignorant. I sometimes wondered how he got to his rank, being so nonchalant and all. It really did grind my gears when he was like that.

I'd rather be stuck with Bobby than the lieutenant. I'd at least learn new things from Bobby, considering I barely knew him, and I wouldn't have to carry him around because he didn't have an old battery.

After a while, I could no longer see the fire, but I was still thinking about it. It was such a random thing to see in the middle of a tunnel. I tried to puzzle out what its function was, and the only thing I could think of was the warmth it gave, but that didn't make any sense. That creature seemed to be doing fine in the cold dark room where we encountered it.

That fire was burning on top of something that looked organic, something I probably should've taken a sample of. I sighed. I had already walked too far, going back would waste too much energy.

I couldn't wait to get out of the tunnels and go home. I was hoping the captain had already sent out a message pod after losing contact, but I knew it was unlikely. Losing contact wasn't a reason to send out a message pod.

The protocol stated that if one were to lose contact with another crewmember, the next in rank had to go and look for the one that is lost. We were only allowed to send out a message pod in emergencies, like if we'd run out of exotic matter, or, in our case, coming across alien life. But the crew in orbit didn't know about the creature we had seen and I feared they were going to send another cognioid to come look for us in these boobytrap-ridden tunnels.

About two hundred meters away from the fire, we came across another divergence of the tunnel. Once again, both tunnels looked exactly the same as the one we were in, with the same repeating inscriptions.

I gave the lieutenant a small bump with my elbow. "Kendrick," I called.

He woke up and opened his eyes, giving his head a little shake. "What is it this time?" he asked. "An iceberg?"

I raised my eyebrows and looked puzzled. "Huh?" I asked. "That doesn't even make any sense."

"It's—" he replied, but cut himself off. "You know what? Never mind. Why did you wake me up this time?"

I nodded my head forward, showing him the divergence.

"Oh," he said, and thought for a couple of seconds. "You choose this time."

I frowned. "Are you joking?" I asked angrily. "I thought you'd at least come up with a better suggestion than that. That's why I woke you up."

"I'm sorry," he said, and shrugged. "But I wasn't trained for a situation like this. Nowhere in our protocol does it say what we should do if we come across two tunnels on a planet infested with aliens."

"Okay, fine!" I shouted. "We'll take the left one, but I'm done carrying you." I let go of his legs and shook him off of my vessel, causing him to fall on his back.

"Ouch!" he yelled, even though I knew he couldn't feel a thing.

"Stop it," I said, looking down on him.

"But why?" he asked.

"I have arthritis."

He stared at me, giving me the *Oh really?* look.

"See? I can be funny too," I said.

"That's quite petty of you, Wendy."

"I don't care. I'm tired."

"Fine," he said, and pushed himself up from the ground. "I'll walk myself. I'm sorry if I did something wrong."

"Well, you should be. This isn't the time to play cool and unconcerned. We might never make it out of here,

Nate."

"You're overthinking this, Wendy. We both have backups at home, and even if we don't make it out of here, they'll send someone down to find us eventually, and let's not forget that we'll get the commendation of discovering this place."

I shook my head. "Gosh, you're always so self-absorbed. I don't want the commendation! I just want to get out of here alive, even if I have a backup."

"And we *will* get out of here alive. They don't leave people behind."

"Cognioids."

"What?"

"We're cognioids. Not people."

"Wow," he said. "And I thought I was the pessimist."

"You know it's true."

"No," he said confidently. "We're still considered people. And if you keep on thinking like that, I might see you as something lesser."

"Never mind."

"Say it."

"Say what?"

"You know what."

"I'm sorry?" I said, confused, thinking that was what he wanted to hear.

"No, although that's actually quite fitting. What I want is for you to admit that I'm right."

That's when I had had enough of his arrogant ass. Instead of saying that he was right, I said, "Fuck off, Nate." I turned my back to him and started walking towards the left tunnel.

"Ouch, that much pride, eh?"

I didn't reply; I knew that was going to give him too much power. I continued walking into the left tunnel, and he eventually followed behind me.

After ten minutes of silence, he tried to talk to me

again.

"I think it was a way to scare us," he said.

"What?"

"The fire. I think that thing tried to ward us off with it."

I thought about it for a second and it actually made a lot of sense.

"And I don't think it's that stupid if it knows how to start a fire," he continued.

"Humans were pretty stupid when they discovered fire," I said.

"Not really. Using something that might hurt or kill you to your advantage, that's actually quite smart if you ask me."

"That's not smart, that's just gutsy; there's a big difference."

"Never mind."

"But not a bad hypothesis," I relented. "This is exactly what I wanted from you," I said, with a small smile.

"To be a genius?"

My smile disappeared and I rolled my eyes at him. "Don't start acting crazy," I said.

He went silent and gave me a cold look. His emotionless face made me believe that I had offended him, but I doubted it. I'd said a lot of worse things to him in the past and he never seemed to care then. Had he finally had enough of me? Did he want me to agree that he's a genius *that* much? I had known him for two hundred years, and not once did he get mad when people questioned his intelligence.

He stayed silent for another minute and frowned. He turned to me and said, "Do you even know why I'm like this?"

"What do you mean? Like what?"

"The way I am," he replied. "My personality."

"Enlighten me."

"Because I know all of you hate me," he said before

turning and walking away from me.

"What?"

"Yeah, don't act like you don't know what I'm talking about. I know all of you have something against me."

I shook my head. "It's not like that. We respect you. It's just that sometimes you—"

He cut me off, asking, "Act crazy, right?"

"I was going to say give off a weird aura."

"What is *that* supposed to mean?" he asked, annoyed.

"It means you can be a real asshole sometimes, Nate."

"Because you guys treat me like one!" he shouted, sighing deeply. "You know what? Just drop it. And just so you know, I wasn't always like this."

"I-I'm sorry," I muttered.

"I said drop it. I don't need any pity apologies."

"I'm not pitying you. I'm genuinely sorry."

He looked at me, clearly angry. "I said drop it!" he shouted, then continued walking, but now at a faster pace, doing his best to leave me behind.

I was flabbergasted. I had never seen this side of him before. I figured it must have been the pressure of being trapped in the tunnels that made him open up. Wait. Was he actually scared of being trapped down here?

I caught up with him and attempted to break the tension with a joke. "So, that thing you shot," I said, "it kind of resembles the captain don't you think?"

He didn't say a word, but the pace of his walking gradually slowed down.

"You know," I continued, "you're going to have to say something eventually."

He sighed. "Can't we just drop this? I'm really tired."

I nodded. "Okay, I understand."

"Thank you."

"Do you need me to carry you again?" I asked.

He shook his head. "Nah. It's fine. I'm in the mood

to walk, it's better if we have two active pairs of eyes anyway."

"How much energy do you have left?" I asked.

"About sixty percent."

"Can I see?"

"No."

"You're lying to me, aren't you?"

"No."

"Then why won't you show me?"

"Because I don't want to."

"I'm really sorry if I hurt your feelings before, Nate," I said. "But you know it's best that I carry you if you're losing too much energy."

He stopped. "Fine," he said, and climbed roughly onto my back again. He dropped his head on my shoulder, causing a small clunk, and powered down. It was like carrying a small child who was pouting because they had been told no.

Carrying him while he was powered down gave me time to think about how we ended up in the tunnels. I didn't believe it was a coincidence that those wrong coordinates happened to lead us to a planet with alien life. Someone back in HQ must've already known about this place. But what I didn't understand was how they knew that we were going to break the law and attempt to mine this planet and not just jump back home.

After a while of walking and getting lost in my own thoughts, I started to miss the others and the jokes we made with each other. I couldn't do that with the lieutenant, especially not after I had maimed his feelings.

I remembered something Vanessa once told me that I found hilarious, the story of how she lost her virginity. I know it wasn't something to laugh about, but I couldn't help it. She had lost it on a ship!

She told me that it was with another woman, someone she thought she loved, but in hindsight, she realizes she didn't.

I happened to be lucky to lose mine to someone I *did* love, and what made it more genuine was that we weren't just attracted to each other because of appearances; it was his soul I fell in love with. Every word he said, every little thing he did, even his breathing made me obsess about him. I suppose I should be glad that I had that experience before getting trapped in a maze full of weird-looking aliens. Although, I suppose in this case they were the natives here and *we* were the aliens.

I was very eager to see what the analysis of their blood said. Judging by the environment it was living in, I was pretty sure that thing wouldn't be able to withstand any form of light, not even starlight.

After a bit, the temperature started changing again; it was dropping this time. I didn't think too much about it; we were walking away from the fire; of course it would be colder this way.

I'd play music if it wasn't going to wake up the lieutenant, and if it wasn't going to drain my battery. I know the whole crew disliked my music, and I don't blame them—it's music from the age of corrupted data over two hundred thousand years ago. The tunes were severely outdated, but I still really liked them, though I couldn't tell you the title of a single song. Because of the data corruption, that information wasn't available. But I didn't care about the titles. I was fascinated by the fact that people used physical instruments to generate music in that age. Making music was truly an art back then, and I found it astounding. Music nowadays is generated by algorithms that try to predict what'll make more credits. It isn't an art anymore; it's more like a business, which didn't exist anymore because the government owned everything.

My favorite song is, I think, called "Why Don't You Do It Right?" by a woman I don't know the name of. I searched every corner of every database to find out who the singer was, but I couldn't find a thing. The song makes me wonder what life used to be like when it was written, especially compared to the way life is now. Men probably used to bring home the bacon in those times; now, the responsibility is split equally, which isn't a bad thing, but it is nice to have someone take care of you once in a while, especially as a vulnerable human.

I kind of missed being one, even though my functionality was severely limited back then. The one thing I missed the most—besides the sex—was coffee. I was very addicted to it. I still was as a cognioid, to be completely honest, but I couldn't drink it like I used to. What I *could* do was activate the part of my mind chip that let me relive the experience of drinking coffee. It was kind of the same, but not entirely. There was something unique about making your own coffee, seeing it, tasting it, and feeling it slip down your throat. I sometimes went out of my way just to make coffee and activate the experience, but then I'd throw the coffee away and feel bad about wasting it afterwards. *Such* an agonizing problem I have.

Our forefathers would've looked at us with disgust if they knew what kind of difficulties we faced today.

Nevertheless, we humans had done quite a good job. No wars, no hunger, no scarcity of resources, the successful colonization of countless planetary systems, *and* we've just recently discovered alien life. It might not be intelligent life, but, truthfully, that could be a very good thing for us.

I had seventy-one percent of my battery's juice left after I walked three hundred meters into the new tunnel. Seventy-one percent gave me thirty-four hours of walking. If I walked a hundred meters a minute, I'd be able to travel about two hundred and four kilometers. Surely, that would be more than enough to find an exit.

The tunnels *had* to have an exit other than the one we came in through. Tunnels without exits would be very impractical. Who would build such a thing without a way to get to the surface?

Chapter 13
The Lieutenant's Past

After a while, I noticed that the temperature had levelled out and was about the same as when we first encountered that thing, which might not have been a coincidence, so I kept my guard up and woke up the lieutenant.

"Lieutenant," I whispered.

"Are we going to make it a regular thing where you ask me to power down and wake me up thirty minutes later?"

"I'm sorry, but I think we might be coming up on that creature again."

"Why do you think that?"

"The temperature," I said. "It's almost the same as when we first encountered the being."

"How do you know their presence is associated with the temperature?"

I shook my head. "I don't, it's an assumption. Don't you think it's smart to start being a bit more cautious?"

He crawled off my back and started to stretch his lower limbs on the dirt—even though cognioids didn't need to do that. We didn't have muscles that would get stiff. "I think it's a waste of energy," he replied, while doing lunges. "But I don't want to end up being wrong about this." He then stopped his stretching, walked past me, and started leading the way.

"Great," I said.

I didn't want to wake him up, because I was the one who suggested carrying him in the first place, but it'd be hard for me, as just one cognioid, to engage in combat, especially if I'm carrying someone. It just wasn't practical.

"You still haven't told me," I asked.

"Told you what?"

"How many hours you have left. And don't lie. I need to know in order to plan things out."

He stretched his arm and turned on the little screen to show me the battery indicator. And there it was, the snowy-white number on a black background: fifty-five percent.

"You said you had sixty!"

"I rounded up."

I rolled my eyes and turned away from him.

"I think there's something wrong with my battery sensor as well," he continued. "The indicator doesn't always show how much I actually have left."

"You're kidding," I said. "So, you could power down any minute?"

"Yes."

I didn't say a word and walked on in silence. This was bad news for the both of us. What was I going to do if he powered down? I didn't want to wander alone in these tunnels and carrying him around with me wasn't any better of an option.

"I lied before by the way," he said.

"What do you mean? When?"

"When I said you and the others made me like this."

"Oh. Why would you lie about that?"

"I wanted you to feel guilty, I guess."

"Well, it kind of worked."

"I'm sorry."

"It's okay," I said. I smiled at him; he deserved it. It was a rare moment when the lieutenant apologized.

"But why are you so…" I trailed off, thinking. I couldn't really figure out a delicate way to ask. "The way you are, anyway?" I eventually said.

"It's best if I don't tell you. It's something stupid."

"Might as well tell me now. There's a good chance we'll both die here."

He acted as if he took a deep breath. "Promise me you won't make fun of me," he said, looking me straight in the eyes. "Or worse, stigmatize."

Well now I had to know. What was there to stigmatize? The only thing I could think of that was frowned upon was being wasteful, and of course murder. I doubted that he had killed someone. That was too much, even for him.

He took another fake deep breath, and briefly closed his eyes. When he opened them, he looked at me for a second before saying, "I got hurt as a kid."

That wasn't the answer I was expecting. What stigma was there to being hurt as a child? "What do you mean?" I asked. "Like, by your parents?"

"Yes."

"Oh," I replied. "I'm sorry to hear that, Nate."

"Don't be, you're not the one who caused it."

"A lot of kids get hit by their parents though."

"It was more emotional than it was physical."

"Oh," I repeated.

"Combined with a pre-existing chemical imbalance in my brain, I ended up having a psychotic episode when I was eighteen," he said, startling me to my very circuits.

"You're shitting me!" I shouted, surprised.

"No," he replied, without looking at me as he continued walking.

Oh my god. He was right to be concerned about stigma. Mental issues were severely stigmatized. They had been since mental illness was even a thing. Scientists hadn't been able to cure them because the only way to do that was to use genetic engineering, which was still strictly prohibited, even after two hundred thousand years. This was because some doofus tried to create super soldiers and overthrow a planet in the past.

It all made perfect sense why the lieutenant had such an uneven temperament. A psychotic episode could permanently affect the prefrontal cortex, the part of the brain responsible for personality development. The personality was the one thing you weren't allowed to change after you've been glitzed into a machine.

"Did you recover?" I asked.

"It's why I glitzed," he said. "So, I wouldn't get another episode. I'm basically cured, but there are some things I just can't change."

I nodded. "I understand."

As he continued forward through the tunnel, all I could do was stare at him. I couldn't believe it. All those times we made fun of him; all those times *I* made fun of him.

"I don't know what to say, Nate," I continued.

"There's nothing to say," he said. "Except that life as a human being really sucks." He began to chuckle and shook his head. "We're so limited by our biology."

I smiled. "Those are probably the truest words you have ever spoken in the two hundred years that I've known you."

"Thanks, I guess."

"Do you want to talk about it?" I asked.

"No," he replied. "I've talked it through with my therapists when I was a human and deleted all my traumatic experiences. Like I said, I'm basically cured."

"Okay," I nodded. "If you say so."

"By the way," he said. "Forget what I said about the fire from before."

"Why?" I asked.

"It doesn't make any sense. If those things really did try to scare us with that fire, how did they know we were in that tunnel to begin with? I didn't see any cameras."

"Hidden cameras perhaps?"

"So, you think they're watching us right now?"

I shrugged. "I don't know. Maybe."

"I doubt it. A life form that has invented cameras wouldn't rely on fire to scare off enemies."

"Makes sense," I said. "But what really baffles me is what they eat down here. I haven't seen a single thing that seems edible."

"I have," he said.

"What? When? And where?"

"Didn't you see what they were burning?"

I stopped walking and thought about it for a second. He was right. It was highly plausible. And it was stupid of me not to have thought about that.

"Fuck," I said. "You might be right." I started walking again. "Still though, that thing they were burning looked disgusting."

"Well, they don't seem like the type of aliens that would be after gourmet cooking."

"Natives," I added.

"Excuse me?"

"We're the aliens, they're the natives."

I saw him tilting his head and frowning, thinking about what I had just said. "Huh," he added. "I guess you're right."

"The temperature is staying constant," I said. "Something tells me we're getting very close to where we don't want to be."

"I don't care, I'm ready for whatever is coming. I have a backup, remember? And so do you, so man up, or woman up in your case."

I gave a small chuckle.

"We need a plan," he said.

"Plan for what?" I asked. "I thought we already had a plan: get Bobby and get the heck out of here."

"No, not that. We need to know what to do if we encounter that thing again."

"Oh."

"I say we spread out when we see that thing and blast

it to pieces. I don't give a damn what the protocol says."

I nodded. I completely agreed with him. The protocol we had required a friendly approach, but that protocol was written ages ago, and had never been revised. I assumed that was because we almost gave up on the potential of encountering alien life.

"This place though," the lieutenant continued.

"What about it?"

"It needs a massive remodeling."

"It's definitely creepy, but beautifully unique in a way."

"And the inscriptions. I missed it before, but it appears to be a repeating pattern."

"I know, I noticed that a while ago."

"Whatever they wrote, it must be important if they were repeating it that much."

"We'll ask Vanessa to decipher it once we get back on board. she has more processing power and access to a broader database."

He nodded.

"I wonder what they used to create them," I said. "It's done so neatly."

"It surely couldn't have been done with whatever that thing had for hands. It didn't really seem like the dexterous type."

"Maybe it had help."

"You mean another species?"

"Yeah," I answered. "An intelligent one that got eaten by the stupid, non-dexterous ones."

"That's quite disturbing, Wendy."

"Oh please, it's nothing compared to the kind of porn you watch."

He quickly turned to me with a surprised look on his face, and squinted his eyes. "How do you know—"

But before he could finish his sentence, I said, "I have a friend back at HQ who manages the servers."

He chuckled. "You little bitch."

I burst out laughing, but quickly contained myself. "I'm just kidding," I said, with a grin on my face. "But based on your reaction, I'm guessing I was pretty close in my assumption?"

"Whatever," he said, and turned away from me again.

"So, what kind do you watch?"

"I'm not telling you," he snarked. "Go ask your friend."

"Oh, come on! I was just kidding. I don't know anyone who manages the servers."

He sighed. "If it means that much to you."

"It does."

"I have a picture of *you* as a human that I use."

I raised my eyebrows. "You're kidding, right?"

"Of course, I'm kidding!" he yelled. "I'd never be attracted to you. I'm out of your league."

I rolled my eyes once again, this time making sure he saw me do it.

"Do you miss being a human?"

"Sometimes," I answered. "I miss the coffee."

He looked back at me with a *really?* sort of look on his face. "From all the things you could've chosen, you choose coffee?"

"Hey, coffee has been around since the beginning, there has to be a reason for that, and I'm assuming it's because it's so damn good."

"Black holes have been around longer than coffee, and I don't think it's because they're 'so damn good'."

I cocked an eyebrow at him, even though he wasn't looking at me. "How about you?" I asked. "Do you miss anything?"

"I was suicidal most of my human life, so no."

"Sorry."

He didn't say a word after that and another awkward

silence ensued. Nothing that came to mind seemed appropriate to break the silence, so I just kept quiet and followed him.

Chapter 14
Eject

We walked five hundred meters before we reached the end of the tunnel. While it only took ten minutes, the awkward silence made the walk feel like a century. At the end of the tunnel, we came to a door that looked exactly the same as the other doors, except this one was slightly open.

"So, what's our plan?" I asked quietly.

"What do you mean?" he asked, as if the plan was obvious. "We go in of course."

I nodded. "I really hope there is a ladder to the surface behind that door."

"With Bobby right next to it."

"Since when are you so considerate?" I asked.

"Since when did you stop?" he asked.

I rolled my eyes at him once again. I had done that so many times by now it was becoming somewhat of a reflex.

"I'm just messing with you," he said after he saw me rolling my eyes. "But stay sharp. We don't know what's behind that door." He crept to the door and looked through the sliver of the opening. "It's an empty room," he whispered.

"Do you see anything that might look like an exit?"

"No, but I see three other doors," he said, and opened the door completely.

We strolled into the room in the direction of the doors, stood in the middle of the room, and looked around. It was just like the last room we were in—the one where we encountered that creature—but less broad, and with one less door.

The lieutenant was standing to my left, analyzing the room—not that there was anything interesting to analyze.

"So, which one do we go in?" I asked.

"The first one on the left."

"Again?" I asked. "Last time we went into the left door, Bobby got split in two pieces."

It took him a second to realize that, and I saw his eyebrows slowly raising up. "Fine," he said. "You choose."

"I think the one on the—"

And that's when I saw something. Behind the lieutenant, at the very right of my visual field. The first door was moving. I hoped it was a shift in pressure between rooms that had caused it, but it continued opening.

I quickly pulled the lieutenant out of the way and back over to the door we had just come through. I nodded at the door that was still opening by way of explaining my actions. When he saw it, he quickly readied his weapon and I followed suit.

We waited for whatever was behind that door to open it completely and come inside so we could blast it to pieces, but when the door was halfway open, the second and third doors started opening as well.

I immediately started to panic and put all my focus on the doors in front of me.

Three versus two. Not very fair, but that wasn't the worst part. The worst part was that it was only a guaranteed *minimum* of three. There could be countless numbers of those creatures about to storm the room. Though my panic continued to rise, I took what solace I could in the fact that we had weapons.

When the doors were fully opened, I expected to see the same creature that we saw back in the other room, and my expectation was met. Four of the things came out, looking identical to the one from before, but it wasn't the number of creatures that caught my attention, it was what they were holding.

They held long, pipe-like structures, about the length of an elephant's trunk, with a narrow end on one side and a bulky end, which their claws were holding onto, on the other. I couldn't believe what I was seeing. I didn't *want* to believe it. It was like our worst nightmare had come true. They were holding weapons.

"Fire!" I heard the lieutenant scream, and immediately saw a plasma charge leaving his cannon. The first two charges missed and hit the area above the first door, barely missing one of the creatures. The lieutenant was a good shot, so I figured his miss was most likely due to the heat-seeking aiming sensors on the cannons not working properly. The creatures must've been cold blooded.

The third charge that the lieutenant fired went right for the creature that came out of the first door. *This is it*, I thought. This will scare the crap out of the other three and will cause them to retreat. The charge went by fast, going right for the head. And it would have been a fatal blow, except that right when it was about to hit one of the eyes of that creature, it was deflected by some sort of barrier. Shit! They had invisible shields!

The lieutenant stopped firing. "Fuck me!" he said.

That's when the four creatures made their move. They didn't fire back on us, but simply looked at one another, as if they were communicating without talking. After a moment, they turned to us and raised their weapons.

The lieutenant put his hand on my shoulder and very slowly said, "Run."

We quickly moved for the door behind us, which we knew was close. The lieutenant went through first, and I followed right after, but just as I was almost through the door, I heard something firing behind me. One shot. It sounded like a bee passing right behind my head.

We both managed to get fully behind the door and

the lieutenant immediately pushed his back against it, using all his weight to force it closed. I wanted to help, but something was wrong.

I was laying on the ground, unable to move my legs and arms. I immediately brought up my system information where I notice that the components tab was blinking. I opened the tab and there it was, blinking in red: my motherboard and my battery were in trouble. I had been hit.

"Fuck!" I yelled. "It got my battery pack and a part of my motherboard. I might malfunction any time, Lieutenant."

"Don't worry, just stay calm. If that happens, I'll still be able to recover your mind chip."

"Lieutenant," I called. He was still standing with his back against the door.

"Not now, I'm busy."

"You won't be able t-t-t-to fight t-t-t-hem," I said, my speech starting to malfunction. "You need t-t-to remove my chip now and run. It's our last chance."

"Fuck!" he shouted.

"I'm unlocking the flap and ejecting t-the chip, so you won't h-h-h-have to do it m-m-manually," I continued. "And don't forget t-the samples I t-t-took.

I browsed through my system menu, making my way to the mind chip menu, where the *eject mind chip* option was located. It was the third option, below *back up* and *defragment*. I selected it, and a small window appeared.

CAUTION: Ejecting your mind chip will cause you to lose consciousness and expose your mind chip. Do you wish to proceed?

I selected yes.

Part IV

Nate Kendrick

The Lieutenant

Chapter 15

The Tunnel On the Right

My back was against the door, ready to stop them from pushing it open. I waited. A whole minute passed by, but I couldn't feel a single thing. Why weren't they attempting to open the door? Had they given up? Did they retreat?

Whatever they were going to do, I wasn't going to wait and find out. I moved away from the door and over to Wendy's powered down vessel.

Turning her head to look at the back of it, I could see the flap that covered the mind chip was open and a part of the chip was sticking out.

Quickly and carefully, I grabbed the chip between my thumb and index finger and pulled it out. I then turned her on her back and opened the compartment in her chest, and grabbed the four containers that contained the specimens she had collected.

I put everything in my own chest compartment, including Wendy's mind chip. I then took the plasma cannon from her shoulder and put it in my bag.

When I had everything, I bolted back in the direction we came from, running as fast as I could, far away from those creatures.

As I distanced myself from them, my mind kept returning to their weapons. They didn't seem primitive, and the shields that protected them had deflected our plasma charges. How was that even possible? Plasma charges were as hot as a star's core. Things were getting weirder the longer we stayed in these tunnels. I had to get out of here as quickly as possible and make sure a message pod was sent—if the captain hadn't done that already.

About halfway through the tunnel, I started to slow down and figured I should check my battery.

Forty percent. That was all I had left. It wasn't a lot, and the faulty battery sensor made everything worse. There was a chance I could power down any minute.

There was only one way that I could go now: the tunnel on the right at the last bifurcation. All the other ways were blocked off or had weaponized aliens in them.

While pacing towards the bifurcation, I started wondering again about the aliens—or natives, according to Wendy. Why did they have such advanced technology, but have doors that unlocked with a simple rotating mechanism? It didn't make any sense, and more questions kept coming to mind the more I considered it. Why did they live underground? Had they also developed faster-than-light travel? And the biggest question: how had they known we were in that room?

It started to make sense to me now why the protocol for first contact was to take a peaceful approach first. It wasn't only to protect *them*; it was to protect ourselves as well.

I had underestimated the natives. I hadn't been concerned about any kind of war with them at first but seeing the kind of technology they possessed made me wonder if they actually stood a chance against us. Or worse. I wondered if we stood a chance against *them*.

Making my way further into the tunnel, I looked back every now and then to see if anything was chasing me, but I was safe. Either they were really slow, or they hadn't bothered following me. I preferred the latter.

I started worrying about Wendy. Her vessel was still back there near those natives. Was it dumb of me to leave it behind? An intelligent species wouldn't hesitate to get their hands on alien technology to study it, but luckily for humanity, those creatures wouldn't be able to get their hands on Wendy's mind chip, which contained extremely valuable information about our own species and our technology.

After another couple hundred meters, I had finally reached the bifurcation.

Quickly, I entered the tunnel on the right, and hoped to God that there weren't more of the natives in there.

I checked my battery indicator again. Thirty-five percent. The rate at which my battery was draining had increased. What a great problem to have when being stuck underground in tunnels filled with mysterious beings.

The day kept getting worse. I had no idea what I was doing, Wendy's and Bobby's lives were in my hands, and I also didn't know where I was going, and what to expect when I got there.

After a while, something about the tunnel caught my attention. It seemed to be going in a circle. If that was the case, that was great news. It meant it was going towards the direction of the entrance!

It was the first positive thing to happen on this whole mission. I checked my magnetometer. It started acting a bit weird again which told me I was right. That weird structure that caused the magnetic interference was close to the entrance, so I was going the right way.

There was one problem, however; if the tunnel led to the entrance, bypassing the first wall that fell, it would mean I wouldn't be able to recover Bobby's chip. I would have to go up as fast as possible, quickly send out for help, and hope *they* could recover the chip. That's all I could do for now. Walk and hope.

But walking alone gave me more than enough time to overthink. I started wondering if telling Wendy my medical history was such a good idea. The last thing I wanted was her telling the whole crew about it. I only told her out of impulse and didn't think it all the way through. I might not be able to get a psychotic episode anymore, but the stigma around mental illness hadn't subsided in over two hundred thousand years.

Humans may have evolved, but their attitudes towards each other had only changed as much as the lizard part of our brain wanted us to. I suppose it was necessary for us to have that. Banter did strengthen relationships, and a civilization where everyone is super friendly to each other seemed kind of delusional, which, funnily enough, was one of my delusions during my psychotic episode.

Another thing that I thought was total bullshit was that we still weren't allowed to use genetic engineering.

You'd think we'd be smart enough by now to know that preventing diseases with gene technology is better than treating them. All that wasted potential just because some weirdo wanted his own planet.

After a couple of hundred meters, I came across another bifurcation. One tunnel went in the direction of the magnetic disturbance, and the other branched in the opposite direction. I chose the former.

I had already come up with a plan at this point, or two plans, really. If I ended up in the tunnel across from that first wall, I'd do what I had said before and just go back up, send for help immediately, go home, and quit my job forever. I didn't want any part of this anymore.

If I ended up on the other side of the wall, I would get Bobby's chip and do what Wendy came up with: stay behind that wall and power down; it didn't seem like a bad plan to me anymore, but that was because I had seen what the natives were capable of, and I had no other options left. I could power down any minute, and I didn't want that to happen anywhere near the natives.

Thinking about getting out of the tunnels excited me, but I also felt more anxious the more I walked the tunnel, because what laid up ahead was a mystery.

It was almost as if this place made to scare things away. The dreadful silence, the long, pitch-black tunnels, and the foul-looking creatures with weapons. I felt like I was in a horror movie, which was my least favorite genre.

The engineers that made our vessels kept our ability to experience fear intact. It helped us survive and make better decisions.

We did have a limiter installed, though, so that we'd never be able to experience something like a panic attack, which was considered pathological.

I checked my indicator again, twenty-five percent left. That meant I had about twelve hours—not factoring in the faulty battery sensor—to complete one of the plans.

It felt like I had been walking forever, but my magnetometer was still acting up the more I walked the tunnel, although not as weird as it had been when we were standing right next to that magnetic structure, so that meant I was nowhere near that thing. I wasn't even sure if I could call that thing magnetic because it didn't have any effect on us cognioids, and we were made out of metal. I figured it had something to do with the planet's magnetic field, but I could've been wrong.

Chapter 16

A New Mission

At the end of the tunnel, I came across another door where the magnetic interference got stronger, but I still wasn't close to that structure. I was ninety-nine percent sure of where that door would lead to though. I approached it quickly, slowly opened it up, and sure enough, it was the room where we had encountered and shot that first creature. It was the room with four doors, and the door I had opened was the second door from the left, right next to the one where the wall fell on Bobby.

This was good news because it meant I could recover his chip. The bad news, however, was that I probably wouldn't be able to get out of the tunnels and would have to stay behind the first wall that had fallen and power down.

I approached the first door from the left, opened it, and there it was: half of Bobby. The wall had crushed the lower half of his vessel, starting from the waist, and had even gotten parts of his arms.

It was unfortunate that this happened to him, but at least he was fortunate enough not to have had his mind chip crushed.

When I was about to approach his vessel, something caught my eye. Something that hadn't been there before when we had passed through this same tunnel earlier.

It was in the dirt. A fresh pair of tracks. The same kind of tracks we followed in the very beginning. They appeared to be leaving from the door I had just entered through and were going through the third door.

No, it couldn't be. Did one of the natives beat me to

Bobby? Had they done something to his vessel? Because aside from being cut in half, he seemed okay from where I was standing.

He was laying face up and, from what I could tell, everything seemed to be fine—except the whole missing lower half of his body thing, of course. The natives must've been curious.

I grabbed Bobby by one of his shoulders and pulled, turning him, so I could recover his mind chip located in the back of his head, but what I saw when I turned him fully toward me caused me to freeze. I couldn't believe what I was seeing.

"Fuck!" I yelled, punching the ground as hard as I could, sending dirt flying onto the wall that had landed on Bobby.

The punch caused my battery indicator to drop from twenty-two percent to twenty.

It was Bobby's head. It had been pried open at the back, right where the mind chip was located. It was gone. Bobby's mind chip was gone!

Those motherfuckers knew exactly what they were looking for. They had left everything else and had taken the most important thing. The thing that contained all our protocols, and who knows what else.

I couldn't let them have it. I knew it was my duty as a member of humanity to follow the tracks and get that chip back no matter the cost.

If the natives were as intelligent as I thought they were, it'd be very bad for our species. They already possessed weapons that could destroy our vessels, and shields that could resist our weapons.

The stakes were high. If I were to fail, it could lead to conflict between humanity and these natives. Conflict where they know more about us than we know about them. Fortunately for me, mind chips were highly encrypted; hopefully that would give me some time before they could obtain any valuable information from the chip. It all depended on their technology, though. And how fast they'd be able to decrypt the chip.

When I got a bit more of a hold of myself I realized that Bobby's plasma ray was also missing, but that was the least of my worries. The weapons the creatures carried seemed just as advanced as our own. Besides, the plasma ray could've gotten crushed by that wall for all I knew.

I shook my head at how this whole situation had unfolded. And now this. I couldn't believe that they knew what a mind chip was. And from the state of things—the other parts of Bobby's vessel were completely untouched—it was clear they went straight for the chip.

Realizing that we had severely underestimated these creatures and having no idea what they were capable of scared the shit out of me.

I let go of Bobby's vessel, dropping him on the dirt. I got up and started following the tracks into the third door.

The dumb thing about being a cognioid, especially one in my current situation, was that I couldn't run or walk faster than I already was to get to my destination earlier. Going faster wasn't energy efficient, so I had to walk at a normal pace. But a normal pace was probably best anyway; I might draw attention if I move around too quickly. And now, more than ever, I had to be careful not to get shot in the head. I was the only one who could get our mind chips back to the ship.

With nothing else to do but walk, I started to contemplate my past. I've lived a long and fulfilling life, right?

Eight-thousand years *was* considered long, I suppose. People didn't have the ability to do that in the past, and I had seen and experienced countless things.

I knew I had a backup tucked safely away at home, but it didn't matter. It wasn't me. I had learned so much in the last thirty hours that I felt like a completely different person.

If my backup was to be restored, it wouldn't know anything of what I had experienced down here. The fear of meeting the first alien creature, the sense of dread in these tunnels, none of it. I shook my head and shrugged it off before I could spiral into a state of perpetual negativity.

I walked on, trying to think happy thoughts. Then I noticed something: the inscriptions were different in the new tunnel. It was still going in repeated sequences, but they were definitely different. I shook my head again. This wasn't something I should be concerned with right now, so I didn't think too much about it. I'd leave it for Vanessa to analyze.

Protocol stated that if alien life was ever discovered, two types of ships would be deployed. One would be a military ship, in case the aliens were advanced, had weapons, and were hostile. The other ship belonged to the Research Organization Concerning Alien Life, or ROCAL for short. ROCAL answers to the interstellar government. And while it might have been called an organization, it was still small and relatively poorly funded because we had never found any alien life in our four hundred thousand years of existence. That's why Bobby was so excited about being the first to encounter an alien life form.

After walking a bit more, I started thinking about the natives again. The shields that they had were going to be a big nuisance, so I had to kill those things before they had a chance to deploy their shields, but I had no way of knowing if they had been deployed or not without shooting at them first. What's more, I didn't know where to shoot them to instantly kill them. For all I knew, their brain was in their legs. But I decided that if the time came, I'd take a gamble and go for the head.

It was really quiet in the tunnels. Those creatures didn't seem to make any noise when they moved around, based on what I had seen so far. Not even when that first one got shot and had run off. It was completely silent. I, on the other hand, made a lot of noise when I moved—part of being a cognioid. I had no idea how sensitive the hearing of those creatures was, but I assumed they could hear me moving around. Knowing so little about these things didn't give me much hope of getting out of here alive.

To increase my chances of success, I grabbed the last two plasma rays from my bag, one for each hand to increase my fire power.

I checked my battery indicator again, which displayed sixteen percent. That meant I had eight hours, not factoring in the faulty sensor.

I shook my head in disappointment. It was so stupid of me not to have changed my battery pack, but there was nothing I could do about it now, so I kept walking and thinking.

Based on the discrepancy between the atmosphere of the tunnels and the atmosphere of the surface, I assumed that the creatures couldn't breathe up there.

What I couldn't figure out was what made the surface uninhabitable for them in the first place. Perhaps their species evolved and lived underground for the entirety of their existence? This was plausible seeing as the scouters hadn't picked up anything that seemed artificial on the surface. An intelligent species would have left ruins up there.

The tunnel I was in was the longest one I had walked so far. I didn't understand why they made such long tunnels with such small rooms in the first place. It didn't make any sense. It was inefficient and seemed like a huge waste of space. I had already walked over a kilometer without coming across anything.

Walking so much with no obvious end in sight caused my thoughts to drift to my past again.

Chapter 17

Contemplation

I was born into an abusive family, developed a serious mental illness, worked thousands of years in a meaningless job with absolutely no sense of purpose, and now I was pretty sure that I was going to get my head ripped open by some weird native creatures on an ugly planet.

If my psychiatrist was still alive, he'd be thinking that I was having a mood disorder, with all the swings I was having.

I never liked my second psychiatrist. He was a judgmental and condescending person; not a good quality to have in someone who gets to know every single detail about your life.

And I kind of hated therapy. Not the talking itself, but the fact that I needed it. It felt so belittling, like I couldn't function on my own in this universe.

The medication was even worse. Mental and neurological illnesses are the only groups of diseases that still used medication. All other types of diseases used more advanced technology—like nanotechnology—with high success rates.

I had used one of the newest anti-psychotics. They worked really well for controlling the symptoms of my psychotic disorder, but they had had some pretty nasty side effects. At least I didn't have to use the old ones. Those were considered semi-useless at least a hundred thousand years ago. While they seemed to work for controlling the symptoms in general, it turns out they were based on a completely wrong mechanism; something to do with dopamine regulation.

I was thinking of becoming an academic researcher in mental health, but then I had my psychotic episode and for a couple years after that I was even more lost and suicidal than I had been in years prior.

I lost my desire to conduct research after that. The only way I was able to get a chance to live a disease-free life was to glitz myself into a vessel. Luckily, my abusive family—bless their hearts—left me quite a big sum of credits, which I didn't want to use at first, but my second therapist said it wasn't horrible of me to do so.

Not to sound too braggy, but I was considered a good-looking person as a human, at least by some. The thing is, I didn't enjoy that as much as I wanted to.

I was a realist with a pessimistic twist. When a girl would show interest, I'd immediately think there was something wrong with her, like she was damaged or something. And that's what kept me from really enjoying life as much as I wanted to. I never voiced this to anyone. I knew it was something stupid to be complaining about, being good looking and all. As cheesy as it may sound, I suppose deep down I knew that happiness wasn't all about good looks, credits, and all that other superficial crap.

Even though I had a pretty good grasp of what happiness *wasn't,* I don't think I really know what happiness *is*. In purely scientific terms, I would define happiness as neurons firing a healthy amount of dopamine and serotonin, but in reality, it's a lot more complex than that.

I had had trouble finding happiness as a human and as a cognioid I was still having trouble. You'd think I could just activate the part of my chip responsible for making me feel good all the time, and believe me, I've tried. And it did work. For like a day. But I realized that I didn't want to be the guy that was always super happy. To be completely honest, it's off-putting.

It's been four hundred thousand years since humans first emerged, and we've perfected interstellar travel, terraforming, and whatnot, but one thing is for sure, we keep getting worse when it comes to our own happiness.

It always pissed me off knowing how people treated each other. One solution I thought would actually work would be if every cognioid simply reprogrammed their personality simultaneously, but that wasn't allowed. The government believed that our personality was what made us who we are and crossing the bridge of personality reprogramming would make us more machine than human according to them.

There were still a lot of unsolved issues concerning glitzing, but we were working on it. Unfortunately, it seemed that every time we fixed one issue, a new one would appear. Take deleting traumatic experiences, for example. It was allowed because it was considered a disease to carry around painful experiences, and then the personality issue arose. A group of people believed that having a flawed personality was also a disease, so they thought we should have been allowed to correct that.

Even if we couldn't fix the issues of personality, we did some amazing things in other areas. I wasn't kidding when I said that humans had perfected interstellar travel and terraforming. We could travel lightyears in a couple hours and change the most awful-looking planets into beautiful green paradises in less than a century.

A lot of people thought humanity would inevitably destroy the earth and cause their own extinction, but that never happened. We used to be stupid, but we weren't that stupid.

Chapter 18

The Octagon

After another five hundred meters of walking, I came across another door, which I found slightly opened. I approached it slowly and looked through the opening. There were two natives standing in front of another door, both of them armed.

I couldn't tell if they were carrying any shields. The last ones we fought only carried the tube-like weapons and still had invisible shields. I figured the weapons generated them, but I wasn't sure.

I decided to take a gamble and attack them. Their backs weren't facing me, so I had to quickly enter the room and go for their heads before they could shoot me.

I slammed my shoulder against the door, causing it to swing open, allowing me to quickly barge in. Notably, not one of the natives seemed the least bit startled by the sound I had generated.

Before they could make a single move, I shot the one on the left with the plasma rays, and the one on the right with the plasma cannon on my shoulder. The charges fired went straight through their heads, killing them instantly, causing them to collapse on each other.

That little scuffle made quite a bit of noise, so I stood there for two whole minutes with my weapons drawn, waiting for something to come out of the door that they had been guarding, but luckily for me, nothing came out. Their hearing must be awful; I really had just made a lot of noise.

I crouched down and looked a little closer at the

creatures I had just killed. I saw that they had what appeared to be tiny holes on either side of their head. If these were for hearing, these organs seemed to be poorly developed.

I got to my feet again and looked around. Killing them had gone easier than expected. If they did have shields, they probably had to be activated before they could be used, which was good news for me. As long as I took them by surprised, I'd be able to kill them.

Seeing as they didn't have any clothes, I didn't have to search and pockets to see if they had Bobby's chip. But I wanted to see if the chip was *in* their bodies. To avoid interference for what I was about to do, I took their weapons, and threw them across the room. I then switched my eyesight to x-ray to see if there were any dense objects inside the corpses that matched the shape of the chip. But, as expected, there was nothing.

I did however, get to see their skeleton, which was composed of very thin but dense bone-like structure. It didn't look anything like a human skeleton. I couldn't see anything that looked like organs. I assumed that was because the organs weren't dense enough for the x-ray to pick them up.

I switched my vision back to night mode and continued forward. The door they were guarding was very different from the others I had seen thus far. This door was wider, taller, and had a thicker frame.

What also caught my attention was the thing next to it on the wall. It seemed to be a scanner of some sort, but looked too small to be used on or by any body part of the natives. Looking closer, I saw that it had been tampered with, perhaps broken.

I walked to the door, stepping over the two dead natives. I pushed the door lightly with my shoulder to see if it was open. It moved. Good news for me. I looked through the opening I had made and couldn't believe what I was seeing.

There was light in this room.

But it wasn't being emitted from a lamp or anything similar. It was coming from screens, buttons, and dials; four rows of them in an octagonal-shaped room.

I turned off my night vision, and refocused. They were computers, or at least that was what they seemed to be. They looked vastly different than anything we had ever made, but I could tell by how one of the six natives in the room was controlling the one in front of them, that they were indeed computers.

I was stupid for not expecting them to have such technology. Why else would they steal Bobby's mind chip? To look at under a magnifying glass?

Out of the six natives, only two of them were armed. They were obviously my first targets. The other four were behind the computers, each one managing one row.

The distance between me and the two guards was quite a bit bigger than what had been between me and the last two guards. To make matters worse, the guards in this room were moving around. I was equipped with a targeting system, but it wasn't bright enough in the room for the system to work precisely, and the heat-seeking function didn't appear to work either. These creatures must have a low body temperature.

I could've waited for them to walk closer to me, but I didn't know when that would be, and my battery wasn't going to let me wait much longer.

My best bet was to enter the room quickly and run towards them while shooting at them. That would increase my chances of success, and I technically outgunned them with the two plasma rays in my hands and the plasma cannon on my shoulder, but I was outmanned, or outnatived in this case.

I had ten percent of my battery left, so I had to do this as quickly and efficiently as I possibly could.

Like I had before, I pushed my shoulder into the door, opening it as fast as I could. I ran in the direction of the two natives with weapons while opening fire. I missed them with my first three shots, but I eventually got the one that was the closest to me.

It dropped to the ground.

I then ran towards the second one, who already had its weapon drawn and was aiming at me.

It was only two meters away. I shot at its head, but the plasma charge was deflected.

Its shield had been activated.

He released a white pulse of energy, almost similar to the plasma charges that came out of our own weapons, but with a zooming sound. It hit my cargon chest plate but didn't penetrate it.

I made it to within arm's reach of the native, let go of both of my plasma rays, and grabbed his weapon with my left hand.

I threw a punch at its arm with my right, hoping it would injure him enough to cause him to release the weapon. It worked, but I didn't just injure him, I fractured his limb, causing a faint crack.

Oddly enough, the native didn't make a single noise or expression, but it did release the weapon, dropping it on the ground.

I took another shot at its head with the cannon on my shoulder, hoping his shield would be down. To my luck, it was.

The native fell on the ground with an apple-sized hole in its head.

I quickly grabbed my two plasma rays from the ground and shot at the heads of the remaining four unarmed natives. All of them dropped faster than a feather in a vacuum.

With them out of the way, I proceeded to look for Bobby's chip. I searched every native, starting with the ones behind the computers.

Just like the ones from before, none of them were

wearing any clothes, so all I had to do was scan them with x-rays. I scanned every one of the six natives in the room, from top to bottom, but the chip was not on or in any of them.

I then started searching around the computers. Each row had two drawers, so I looked in those. But again, nothing. It must not be in this room.

I looked around again. There was another door across from the door I had entered through, but I didn't have time for another shootout or another long tunnel. I was running on six percent of battery now.

"I won't be able to fucking do it," I murmured.

I ended up getting so frustrated that I threw a punch into one of the screens, shattering it and revealing the insides hidden behind it.

The components immediately behind the screen were expected, but in the middle was an empty space with a little podium-like structure. It almost looked like a scanner.

I examined the shattered screen more closely and saw that the whole screen could be opened up like a flap.

There was a total of ten screens divided amongst the four rows, so I moved quickly from one screen to the next, opening each of them. By the seventh screen, I had finally found what I was looking for.

Bobby's chip was sat on the little podium surrounded by the mysterious-looking components. This was the first time my lack of control over my anger had actually led to something positive.

I grabbed the chip, opened the compartment in my chest, and put it right next to Wendy's. The natives were most likely analyzing it, but I had no idea how their computers worked or if they had managed to get any information from it.

I also didn't know if these computers were connected to another database somewhere else. If they were, destroying them would be senseless, but I did it anyway. It was the least I could do. I aimed my rays and cannon at all ten screens in the room and shot at them multiple times until there wasn't any light left in the room.

Chapter 19

Tough Decision

After turning on my night vision again, I went back to the door I had entered through. I looked at the indicator on my arm: five percent. That gave me a little over two hours. It wasn't a lot of time, but perhaps enough to go to the first wall that trapped us and power down there.

I opened the door, entered the room, stepped over the two natives I had killed earlier, and walked towards the tunnel I had come in through, but just as I reached the door of the tunnel, I fell to the ground, unable to move my arms and legs.

I had run out of power.

My indicator had said five percent, and there was no warning, which I should have gotten, that I was about to run out of power.

"Fuck!" I yelled, even though I knew yelling would consume more energy.

I could still use my shoulders, so I used those to move through the dirt, until I reached the wall next to the door where I rested my head on the ground.

There was only one thing I could do at this point. The one thing I had hoped I would never have to do, ever. I unlocked the compartment on my chest, and swung my vessel to the side, causing the mind chips to fly out of the compartment, and land on the dirt a meter next to me.

The four sample vials were anchored into the compartment, so they didn't fly out.

I closed the compartment and stared at the chips for

a brief moment, hesitating. Should I really do what I was about to do? I shook my head, started moving the plasma cannon on my shoulder, and aimed it at Wendy's chip.

"I'm sorry, Wendy," I said.

I sighed and closed my eyes.

It took me another second, but I eventually released a plasma charge at her chip, destroying it. What remained of the chip flew a couple of meters away. No data could ever be extracted from that.

I proceeded to aim the cannon slightly to the right, where Bobby's chip was laying.

Destroying Wendy's chip was hard enough, but doing the same to Bobby was torture. And, honestly, it would've been considered murder.

I sighed again.

Looking up, I blamed the only one that could've been held responsible for this sad, miserable life I had been given. "This isn't fucking fair, you fucking prick!" I yelled. My life was such a joke.

"Bobby," I continued. "I know you can't hear me, but please forgive me for doing this."

After closing my eyes again, I released a second charge, causing the chip to fly just like Wendy's. It dropped right next to my vessel. I had destroyed it to the point that only a quarter of it remained.

I had murdered our recruit.

I then turned the cannon, aiming it at my head, which was easy, because it was right next to it.

I started chuckling like the madman I knew I was. My whole human life I had been battling suicidal thoughts. I had used a huge portion of the credits that my abusive family had left me to glitz myself into a vessel so I wouldn't ever think about killing myself again. But here I was, about to shoot myself in the head. Not because I wanted to, but because I had to, for the same people that have judged and looked down on me my whole life.

If this wasn't the finest example of irony, then I didn't know what was. I knew I had a backup at home, but screw that. That back up was still another person in my eyes.

I positioned the cannon right where my mind chip was located and proceeded counting down from three. When I reached zero, I closed my eyes, and started screaming as loud as I could.

"Argh!" I yelled, and then everything went black.

Part V

Erma van Hout

The Commander

Chapter 20

Forty-Four Hours

The captain and Vanessa were still going at it. Two hours had passed since we lost contact with the others on the surface, and we couldn't come to an agreement on what we had to do next. There was no protocol for our specific situation, one that said what the next step was if we lost contact with crewmembers on a planet that was *probably* infested with aliens, and with one of the members not being backed up.

The captain seemed to be holding it together, but I could tell he was worried sick. Vanessa, on the other hand. wasn't afraid to show her emotions. She sounded like a mess.

"We can't send a message pod because there isn't a single piece of evidence that there's anything alive down there," the captain said to Vanessa. "That's what one of the protocols says"

"You're just saying that because you're scared of getting into trouble," Vanessa snarked.

"What kind of trouble could I possibly get into for sending a message pod?"

"For starters, the use of exotic matter for the pod," Vanessa answered. "And secondly, the fact that you went off course to mine an unknown planet."

"I don't give a rat's ass about that," the captain said. "No evidence. No message pods. That's what that protocol says and I'm going with it."

"I know, but that protocol isn't doing us any good right now. We need to send for help! Bobby could be on the brink of death at this very moment."

"We've had this conversation already, Vanessa," the

captain added. "It's only been two hours since they went underground. Bobby's battery pack will last him another forty-six, forty-four if you count the extra two hours that they spent on board."

"Send the pod, Lester," Vanessa demanded.

"No," he replied firmly. "And what's with calling me by my first name?"

"We can't just wait around and do nothing."

It was then that I intervened. "Vanessa is right," I said.

"Okay," the captain said, and turned to me. "What do you think we should do?"

"We have no protocol for our specific situation, right?" I asked.

The captain nodded.

"But we can still follow the one concerning missing crewmembers," I pointed out. "I say we go into the tunnel ourselves and see why they aren't responding. This way we're still following your precious protocols."

"You know the one next in line to enter is you, right?" he asked me.

I nodded. "Yes."

He sighed lightly. "Here's what we'll do," he said. "We'll wait the other forty-four hours and if they don't show up, you can go in to look for them. Even if they run out of power, you'll still be able to recover their mind chips."

"But what if they're in trouble right now?" Vanessa asked immediately. "Bobby's life is literally on the line here."

"Stock frames and body plates are strong enough to withstand a thousand newtons of force," he replied. "I'm sure he's doing fine."

"His life is your responsibility, Captain," Vanessa snarked at him. "You know that, right?"

The captain didn't bat an eye at her hologram. "My decision is final," he said with a straight face. "We'll regroup on the bridge in forty-four hours, or when we hear something from them. This discussion is over, am I clear?"

"But forty-four hours is too—"

"Am I clear?" the captain repeated, cutting Vanessa off.

"Yes, Captain," she replied.

He turned to me, expecting my concurrence. "Commander?"

I nodded. "Yes, Captain."

Satisfied, he left the bridge.

I had never seen him act like that before. This was one of the rare moments where we couldn't persuade him; granted, we were under very unique circumstances. He knew Vanessa was right and that we didn't have to wait that long to actually do something, especially considering someone down there wasn't backed up.

I looked over at Vanessa's hologram. She seemed very disappointed and looked as if she wanted to fly the ship to the surface and rescue them.

"Don't fight it," I told her. "I understand why you're upset, but he is our captain."

"I know that, but he's making decisions out of fear at the expense of the others."

"I know, but let's not forget that they're still cognioids. *Heavily armed* cognioids."

"What if there's actually something down there?"

"Think about it, Vanessa. Something that lives in underground tunnels couldn't possibly stand a chance against cognioids."

"Fine, I'll just wait it out then, but I still think Captain Pierce isn't thinking straight."

"There's nothing we can do. We need to follow his orders."

He wanted hard evidence of alien life before we were going to send out a message pod, but in my opinion, the tunnel itself was more than enough evidence. There was no way that it was a natural phenomenon.

Just like Vanessa, I too thought the captain was worried he'd get in trouble for trying to mine a planet he wasn't supposed to, even if he claimed he didn't care. I don't know what he was planning on doing. We'd have to report the tunnels eventually, so he'd get caught no matter what.

I felt like I needed a break from everything, something to distract me for the next forty-four hours out of waiting.

The problem was that I didn't have anything to distract myself with. Being a cognioid made absorbing information instantaneous. Take eBooks, for example. I liked reading them, but I could read a two hundred thousand word novel in less than a nanosecond. Unless I had an actual paper book to read, which had become super rare. Almost nobody printed books anymore, and it wasn't because of environmental issues—we solved those problems ages ago—it just wasn't efficient to go through the printing process for a book that would be read in hours.

You might be wondering about humans who haven't glitzed and how they absorbed information. And yes, while it was true that human brains were significantly slower at absorbing information, they could still get an Encephalink, a brain-computer interface, something almost everybody gets installed. It was basically like putting your brain on steroids. Anyone that didn't get one installed fell behind drastically. It was a no-brainer—no pun intended—to get one. The government installed them, and it was free. Those who refused to get one were usually protestors, typically religious people, but they were the ones that needed it the most in my opinion.

The same problem I had with books, I had with movies. I could play them in my head in less than a second and recite the whole thing for you. Being a cognioid might have a lot of perks, but it wasn't as enjoyable as some people might believe.

"Can you recommend an activity for me, Vanessa?" I asked. "You know, to keep me distracted."

"How about a videogame?" she asked me.

"I'm not in the mood to enter any virtual world."

"I was thinking of something more ancient."

"I'm listening," I continued, curious.

"It's a puzzle game."

"What year is it from?"

"That's the thing," she said excitedly. "Nobody knows! It's from the era of corrupted data. I couldn't even find the name. It was salvaged and reconstructed by some friends of mine back on earth. I think it's from the thirtieth century."

"Is it installed in your drive?"

"You bet. I've already played it a couple of times."

"Alright, run it, let me see."

She used the big front window of the ship to display the game and showed me how it was played. The player had a gun that could generate portals, and you had to find a way to get out of rooms, by using the portals to solve puzzles. It was intriguing.

"The graphics look like it's a game from the twenty-first century though," I commented.

"That's what I thought as well," she said, "But the gameplay seems like it's of the thirtieth, and I've heard that people in the thirtieth century were really obsessed with retro graphics."

"Alright, and it's not a VR game?"

"No."

"Then how do I control it?"

"With this," she said, popping open a drawer. There was a black device inside that looked like nothing I had never seen in my life. It had colored buttons and some weird little mushroom sticks that toggled in every direction. From the top a cable ran into the drawer. I grabbed the device and pulled on it.

"Don't!" she yelled. "It has to be attached."

I looked at the device, turning it in every direction, and inspecting every corner of it. "What the hell is this?" I asked.

"It's a gaming controller, and it's very ancient. I had to pay good credits for this thing. It was from a very old digital blueprint that was reverse engineered by one of my friends back home."

"How do I use it?"

"I don't know. You have to learn as you use it."

"Wait, why did you buy it if you don't even have hands to control it?"

"I bought it because I'm a collector. I have a whole storage unit back home full of ancient technology. *And* I sometimes bring friends on board to play this game."

"Alright. Let's try it out then," I said as I pulled out a chair to sit in front of the window.

I played the game non-stop for about twelve hours, while Vanessa watched and walked me through the more difficult puzzles. The game itself had a story arc, which was admittedly well written. After I finished the game, I put the controller back in the drawer.

"So, what do you think?" Vanessa asked me.

"Oh. It's actually pretty good."

"I knew you'd like it."

"Well, I'm all gamed out, and we still have about thirty-two hours left. Do you have any other things I might like?"

She shook her holographic head. "Not really," she said. "If I had known you were going to ask me for entertainment, I'd have backed up more games onto my drive."

"Was that the only game you backed up?"

"Yeah. I know it looks weird to only back up one game in a massive drive, but it's my favorite one, and I don't like digital clutter."

"It's fine. I understand. But I do think it's weird knowing you have people on board this ship besides us."

She chuckled. "Of course," she said with a grin on her face. "I have social needs you know. I'm not a machine."

I gave a small giggle. "Yeah, sorry I asked. Just never crossed my mind. I think I'm going to look for other ways to keep myself busy."

"Alright."

I walked to the center of the bridge, and sat down on one of the chairs, trying to figure out what else I could do. That was a pretty fun game. It was, however, a huge waste of time. People apparently loved that sort of thing two hundred thousand years ago.

Thinking about it, I couldn't help but chuckle at how ahead of its time the game was. One of the characters was a woman who had her mind transferred into a machine. She was very controlling and used humans as her test subjects, which wasn't quite how things were today. Machines and AI have never rebelled against humans.

Machines and humans have had a symbiotic relationship since the very beginning. They've helped each other improve through things like the Encephalink I mentioned earlier. It made us smarter, which in turn helped human engineers improve technology further. It was how we excelled as a species.

And speaking of species, we've managed to conserve every beneficial living organism since the year fifteen thousand. Even the good bacteria that lived in our digestive tract. We eradicated those that made us sick, like the ones that caused tuberculosis or even small abscesses in our skin.

It was crazy to think how much we had improved healthcare, even if it wasn't in all areas. Genetic engineering—although perfected—was still prohibited for ethical reasons, so some diseases were still hard to treat, especially those that concern the brain and psyche.

Infectious diseases, on the other hand, were so easily

manageable that only a couple cases would crop up each year across all planetary systems *combined.*

And then there was cancer. That one was tricky because it was mostly a genetic disease at its core, and we couldn't use gene-editing, but we were still able to manage that with nanotechnology.

We'd inject nano-sized, programmable, devices into the blood stream of an infected individual. These nanobots would kill all cancerous cells in the body. The treatment had an efficacy rate of nearly a hundred percent without a single side effect—if you discounted the pain of the injection of course. The nano devices were excreted from the body via the kidneys, and could be extracted from the urine to be sanitized and reused.

I tried to brainstorm for activities to keep me busy while we waited but I couldn't think of any so I decided to go to the one place that I always found therapeutic, the hyperdrive. It was one of the greatest, if not, *the* greatest product of the human mind, with a little help of the Encephalink.

It was how we cheated the universe, traveling lightyears in just hours. If there was a god, I bet they would put all humans in Hell simply because we had invented this thing. Although, any type of afterlife was impossible at this point because humans were technically immortal. You'd have to be really stupid to permanently die in this day and age, especially if you were a cognioid.

I got to the hyperdrive room and opened the thick door. This was the smallest room on the ship with the most important device on board. The walls were padded with a material made out of lorunium, which was used to absorb the massive amounts of gamma radiation released during a hyperjump.

The hyperdrive had a small glass window on the center module to allow easier access for diagnostics by the mechanic, but I used it for my therapy. Watching exotic matter be converted into energy was soothing. A small stream of bright golden-red exotic matter as thick as a strand of hair would flow into the middle, right behind the glass window, and as the worm hole was generated, the space and matter around the exotic matter would warp.

It looked like magic.

Knowing I contributed to the science behind this machine by mining negatanium gave meaning to my life.

In standing so close to the drive I was exposing myself to massive amounts of radiation, but that was fine; I wasn't affected by it. All cognioids have any kind of radiation washed away immediately when they return to their designated planet.

Watching the conversion of exotic matter to energy, I couldn't help but think that If I hadn't become a commander, I would have made a great mechanic. Not that we had a bad one, Wendy was a saint, but I'd probably be on a different ship, or perhaps work on a Dyson swarm, which was another great work of art.

While I would have been a great mechanic, I would have made an awful engineer. I knew how machines worked and how to fix them, but I lacked creativity, and had never designed a single thing in my life.

You might be wondering if we were able to simply upload protocols into our mind to make ourselves more creative, but the answer is no.

Creativity was a very complex process, which was mostly based on personality; something we weren't allowed to change.

I sighed to myself. Another five minutes passed as I watched the exotic matter conversion and then the captain walked into the room. "You know, there are people who are professionally trained to help you with your mental health," he teased.

He knew I liked to come here because it was therapeutic. I even let him join me once to see what all the fuss was about, but he didn't get why I liked it so much and had ruined the mood for me. I hadn't invited him back since.

"Very funny," I said sarcastically.

"Look," he said as he put a hand on my shoulder. "I just wanted to talk to you about my decision back on the bridge."

"There's nothing to talk about," I replied. "You're our captain, and we need to follow your orders."

"You understand why I had to make the decision I did, right?"

"Because you're scared?"

"No," he replied quickly, clearly irritated. "Ugh. Look, we can't just call in two ships to jump across the galaxy wasting valuable resources, just on the off chance that there might be alien life on a planet. We need real proof, not just a tunnel that could've been formed by shifting plates. You're a commander of a mining ship, you should know how valuable exotic matter is."

"I do know," I added, moving my shoulder and causing his hand to slip off. "But I also know how valuable the life of a cognioid who hasn't been backed up is."

"Bobby's a cognioid. He's basically immortal. The worst that could happen is that he falls into a pit with an EMP grenade next to him that's about to detonate. And I'm pretty sure they didn't go down there with any EMP grenades."

"I hope you're right, Captain," I said, avoiding his gaze and instead staring at the small glass window in front of me.

"I'll take full responsibility if anything goes wrong, don't worry."

"The problem isn't a matter of who's going to take responsibility. The problem is that Bobby's life is at stake here."

He shook his head in frustration. "You know what!?" he shouted furiously. "I'm getting tired of you all making me out to be the bad guy here. I was the one who told Bobby he could come back to the ship, but he insisted on staying planet side. It's not my fault he's deluded with the idea of finding alien life."

I didn't reply. His outburst had startled me, though I didn't blame him for it. Vanessa and me did keep blaming and pushing him.

He sighed, his shoulders sinking a bit. "Just—just don't think too much okay, Commander?" he said, and walked out of the room leaving me to my solitary therapy session.

I know what he wanted. He wanted the others to appear back on the surface entirely unscathed and with a huge haul of negatanium. Then we could go back home without ever having to report the tunnels.

He was partly right with what he had said, though. We didn't have hard evidence of alien life on this planet. The only proof we had was the one tunnel. And while it looked artificial, it wasn't enough to call in the ROCAL and the army. It had happened before that a crew called them in, but it was a false alarm. The crew had discovered caves that were formed in a weird pattern. They were excited by the find, but when they called in the professionals, it didn't end well for them. The weird patterns they had described turned out to be the formation of what used to be oceans. That crew lost all credibility after that, and some of them were even demoted.

With my mood ruined by the captain, and having nothing else to entertain myself, I couldn't help but want to get into a lander and go looking for the others. I really didn't want to wait in the ship for another thirty-two hours worrying about the rest of the crew. If we hadn't discovered the tunnels, we'd already be done with our mission and traveling back to Earth by now.

The people back home might even be wondering why we hadn't jumped back yet. The thing was, a rescue team wouldn't be deployed unless a message pod had been sent, or until they were certain Vanessa's dark matter had run out, which would've been at least two hundred hours after she had left Earth.

I decided to go back to the bridge and chat with Vanessa again. The hyperdrive wasn't doing anything for me—thanks to the captain.

I was getting tired; not physically since cognioids didn't experience physical fatigue, but I was emotionally wrecked. I kept overthinking and catastrophizing about what may have happened to our crewmates on the planet, and it was hard to stop.

I walked onto the bridge and everything was quiet. The captain wasn't there, and even Vanessa's hologram had been deactivated.

"Vanessa?" I called.

"Yes, Commander?" she replied, and out popped her hologram in the middle of the bridge.

I turned to her with a sad face, showing her how desperate I was, and said, "I'm bored."

"Err...I'm sorry to hear that, Commander."

"Can you keep me company?"

"Sure."

"For thirty-two hours."

She went silent. She clearly thought I was joking. She had other things to do than waste time talking to her commander for literal hours.

"I know, I know," I said. "It's a long time. But either you help to keep me occupied, or I steal a lander and go in the tunnels against Lester's orders."

"Well, in that case, no!" she said, "I don't want to keep you company."

I grabbed the edge of the table that projected her hologram and shook myself from side to side, acting like a toddler demanding something from their parent. "Come on, Vanessa, I'm dying here!" I said as if this was the worst torture in the world. "I thought you were my friend."

"Am I?"

At her question, I stopped, having to think for a moment. "I actually don't know," I said. "I think so. We've known each other for five centuries. That's got to mean something, right?"

"I suppose, but I'm not really a cognioid, so we can't interact that much."

"Well, that game thing we played together was fun."

"I barely did anything, I just watched you play."

"Yeah, but it was fun playing it while you were watching."

"Well, there is a co-op mode."

"Co…op?" I asked in confusion.

"Yeah, like a two-person mode."

My jaw dropped and I just stared at her hologram in disbelief.

"What?" she asked, confused.

"Why didn't you tell me that before!?" I shouted.

"I didn't know you wanted to play *with* me."

"That's bananas!" I shouted. "Come on, let's play! I'll go get the controller."

"You know," she said, "you don't really need a controller. You can do it wirelessly by connecting to my system. Just don't go into the folder called downloads, I have... personal stuff in there."

I stared at her again, arching one of my metal eyebrows. She gave me a look that clarified what she meant by personal stuff.

"Uhm, I think I'll just use the controller, just to be safe."

"Yeah, that's probably better."

"How many times have you played this co-op mode?" I asked as I grabbed the remote from the drawer.

"About thirty times, but I delete my experiences after every time."

"Why?"

"So I can enjoy it again without getting bored.

You've got to take advantage of being a machine every now and then, Erma."

I chuckled lightly. "Yeah, I guess you're right." I sat down, making myself comfortable. "Let's get started."

The co-op mode had the same principle as the single-player mode, except that the puzzles were more difficult to solve, and you had to work together with another person to solve them, which was a bit frustrating at some points.

We completed the co-op mode in fifteen hours. When we were done, shook my head in frustration. "I feel like we could've done better."

"I thought we did pretty well," Vanessa said. "The levels seem significantly more difficult than the ones from the single-player mode."

"That's true, but we had to redo a lot of those levels."

"True, and I by no means blame you," she said sarcastically.

I frowned. "What do you mean by that?" I asked.

"You know exactly what I mean."

"I really don't."

Her hologram frowned and looked very pissed. "You clearly took the longest to solve the puzzles, and if that wasn't bad enough, you were super controlling during the game. I know you outrank me in real life, but this is *my* game, Erma. And we were playing in *co-op* mode. We were supposed to be making decisions *together*."

"Oh, wow," I said. "I'm sorry I made you feel that way, Vanessa. I didn't know this game meant that much to you."

"It's not that!" she shouted. "Ugh, you know what? Just leave it. What matters is that we finished the game."

"Yeah, but how long does it usually take to finish it?"

"I don't know. I deleted past experiences, remember?"

"Right." I stared are hologram for a moment. This seemed like a bit of an overreaction to our playing a game together. "Are you alright?"

"Yeah, don't worry about me. I just have a lot on my mind right now."

"Alright. If you need someone to talk to, you know where to find me."

"Yeah, thanks."

"I'm going to check up on the captain," I said and walked towards the exit of bridge. "We haven't seen him in quite a while."

"He's in the cabin right next to the AVAC," she added in an emotionless tone.

Clearly something was bothering her. I suspected she was getting tired of taking orders as a ship for so many years.

"Alright, thanks."

"No problem," she said in the same emotionless tone.

"And Vanessa?"

"Yeah?"

"I really hope they pass that law. I can't imagine how sick and tired you must be of being a mining ship."

She turned off her hologram, and after a second, I heard her speak through the intercom. "Uh huh."

I left the bridge and headed to the cabins. That was intense. I didn't know she hated being given orders *that* much, but I didn't blame her.

Being a ship had to be hard, especially if you'd been one for eight thousand years. I didn't really want to check up on the captain, I just had to get out of there because it was getting awkward, and I had never handled awkward situations well.

The game was a pretty good distraction, and it helped me bond with Vanessa—albeit not in the healthiest way. Gaming had become a colossal industry. In every planetary system, about three quarters of humans—who hadn't already glitzed—considered themselves avid gamers, most of whom had made a career out of it. And why wouldn't they? Making credits while having fun was a dream job, but burnout among gamers had risen in the past couple of centuries. Experts blamed it on the pressure gamers put on themselves to be the very best in every game they played. That's why psychiatric consultations by gamers had been rising as well. The condition even had its own name: GES, gamer exhaustion syndrome.

I wasn't much of a gamer myself, I played from time to time, but I had a job I already liked and was happy sticking to it.

Just as I was walking into the corridor that led to the cabins, I saw the captain. I wondered to myself how he had so easily kept himself busy for the past twenty-seven hours. There was literally nothing to do on the ship other than talk to each other, and I had kept myself busy with the only other crewmember still onboard.

He turned in my direction right as he left the cabins and started walking towards me.

"Hey," I called to him as he was just about to pass me in the hall.

"Hey, what's up?"

I shrugged. "Nothing really. I wanted to apologize for before. I guess I turned on you because I don't want anything to happen to one of our crewmembers, especially not on their first day."

He nodded.

"So," I continued, "what have you been doing the past twenty-seven hours?"

"Nothing much. Trying to think of a plan for what to do if they really don't show up."

"I thought we already had a plan? I'll go down to look for them."

"Do you really feel like you're up for it? We can go together if you want."

"I can handle myself. I'll ask for your help if it's necessary."

"Alright, just watch your back down there."

"Got it."

"I'm assuming our radio waves can't reach the tunnels, but if you really come across anything that looks alien, you come back up right away, and I'll send a message pod."

"Are you sure? Don't you want to wait for some harder evidence?"

He pointed his index finger at me. "Hey!" he shouted menacingly. "Don't test me."

I couldn't help but chuckle. "I'll do my best, Captain."

"Good to hear."

"Still seventeen hours to go though."

"Yeah, quite a while. We've never stayed so long in another system."

"Yeah, and it's starting to wear on me. Do you know anything I can do to keep myself busy?"

"Not really."

"How are you not bored?" I asked, shaking my head in disbelief.

"I do get bored, but not in situations where my crewmembers are in danger and my career is on the line."

"So, what you're saying is that you're enjoying this?"

"No. What I'm saying is that I don't have time to be bored when I'm worried."

"Oh. I can't really do that; time goes by slower when I'm worrying." I sighed, drooping my shoulders.

"It'll be alright," he said. "We've always pulled through no matter the situation, right?"

"Yeah, but the biggest problem before now was a harvester falling into an acidic ocean. This is worlds apart."

"I know, but if we reach a point where we don't see a way out of this, we'll send a message pod. It's that simple. Try to mentally prepare yourself for when you get down there, okay? It's good to be prepared."

“I’ll try. For now, though, I think I’m going to look for another distraction.”

“Why don’t you just power down in your hibernation station and wake up when it’s time?” he asked. “You won’t have to worry during that time, and you’ll be fully charged when you wake up.”

I nodded. “You could’ve told me that twenty-seven hours ago, Lester,” I blamed him before walking to the hibernation stations next to the AVAC.

He shrugged, and walked the other way, turning into the corridor that led to the bridge.

He was right. Powering down was the most logical thing to do. I didn’t think about it because we only ever used the hibernation stations at the start of missions so we’d be fully charged, and my mind was fixed on the rest of the crew. I was going to have to charge up before going on the planet anyway. If I had just thought of using my hibernation station from the beginning, it would’ve spared me from the awkward conversation with Vanessa.

I walked past the AVAC and turned left into the room that had the six hibernation stations.

My station was the second from the right, between the captain’s and the lieutenant’s. Each station had anchors that would prevent us from moving or falling off in case we had a bumpy ride—which almost never happened. Located in the middle of the station was a wireless charger that allowed us to fully charge our batteries in a couple of minutes.

I got into my station, wirelessly activated it, and the anchors snapped on around my wrists, shoulders, waist, and ankles. I could see my battery indicator quickly rising from forty percent. I then set my internal timer to seventeen hours, and powered down, causing my vision to go black, my hearing to go deaf, and depleting my consciousness to nothing.

Chapter 21
The Vanishers

Seventeen hours passed and I woke up automatically. We didn't have the same grogginess that humans often experienced after waking up, so I felt exactly the same as before I had entered the hibernation station.

The anchors released my vessel, allowing me to push myself out of the station. I walked into the corridor, and headed towards the bridge.

There, the captain was sitting in the chair he always sat in at the only table on the bridge, but he was doing something I had never seen him do before: he was reading a *paper* book. I curiously zoomed in on the title, *Stellar Civilization: The Art of Colonizing Other Systems*, by Engle Pobius.

When he noticed me, the captain placed an old, torn bookmark at the page he had been reading, closed the book, and placed it on the table. "We've been waiting for you to wake up," he said.

"Don't you think it's a waste of time to read a physical book?" I asked as I walked towards him, taking a seat in one of the free chairs. "What were you reading anyway? I don't know that one."

"I think it's better to read than to play a game for twenty-nine hours," he said with a teasing tone. "And it's a very old book. I doubt you'll know it."

Vanessa's hologram immediately popped up with a furious look on her face. "It was twenty-seven!" she shouted.

He rolled his eyes. "Sorry," he said unapologetically.

"Anyway," I cut into their conversation, preventing

it from erupting into another unnecessary argument. "Have you heard anything from below?"

They both shook their heads.

"No," the captain said. "And I don't think we will. It's already been forty-eight hours since they woke up from hibernation. They'll have to have powered down by now."

I nodded. "Do I still need to go into the AVAC before entering a lander?"

"No, that's fine," the captain answered. "You were analyzed when we entered the system, right?"

"Yeah."

"Alright then," Vanessa said. "Do you feel ready?"

"Not really, but I need to do this."

"I can still join you if you want," the captain added.

I shook my head. "There's no need," I said. "Besides, the protocol says the lowest ranked *cognioid*, and not *cognioids*."

"Just be safe, okay, Commander?" he said empathetically. "And remember, if you see any evidence of life down there, you come right back up and tell us."

"What if I end up staying there, and don't respond just like the others?"

"I already had that conversation with Vanessa," he replied. "If that happens, I'll come get you, and if we all end up stranded down there, Vanessa will send a message pod for help."

"Sounds like a plan. There's probably nothing for us to worry about though. It doesn't seem likely that there's something down there that could harm cognioids."

"Exactly. I think the others probably got lost in that tunnel, rather than injured."

"Wait," I stopped and looked at the captain in confusion. "If that's the case, how will I navigate through the tunnels?"

"Calibrate your magnetometer," I heard Vanessa say. "The others might have forgotten to do that."

I nodded and jumped up from the chair in a striking motion, causing it to fling back. "Alright, let's fucking do this!" I yelled. I paced towards the arsenal, which was located in the room next to the bridge. I pulled down the sliding hatch, took one of the three plasma cannons, and installed it on my shoulder.

The captain caught up with me as I was testing the cannon's stand, moving it in every direction. "Good luck down there, Commander," he said.

"I don't need luck," I added, and started walking towards the landers. The captain followed me.

"Don't get cocky," he continued. "If you encounter anything suspicious, you come right back up." He grabbed my shoulder and turned me to face him, looking me in the eyes. "That's an order."

I quickly broke eye contact, turned back around, and continued walking, causing him to release his hand. "Got it," I whispered.

When I got into a lander, a surge of emotions hit me. It was so overwhelming that I couldn't tell what I was feeling, but one thing was certain: I didn't feel confident. If three cognioids with weapons couldn't handle those tunnels, how would one cognioid be able to?

Vanessa had already put in the coordinates of where I had to land, right near the hole they had drilled.

I wirelessly instructed the lander to initiate, and it detached from the ship and projected towards the planet. When it entered the planet's atmosphere, the lander started to vibrate. I could tell from the vibration that the atmosphere was significantly different than earth's—which didn't cause any vibration at all.

After I landed and the hatch opened, a thick rush of brown smog entered the lander. There was a storm happening.

I pushed the restraints upwards, and stepped foot on the surface. The winds were fast, but not strong. I couldn't see a thing due to the brown smog.

"This…i-is t—" I heard through the radio, the signal was choppy and kept breaking off.

"What?" I yelled back.

"This…i-is t—," I heard again. The storm was interfering with the radio waves, and I still couldn't see a thing. I climbed back into my lander and pulled the hatch down, closing me off from the storm.

The floor of the lander was covered with a layer of dirt, and the walls were smudged with the same. I had no vision out there, and no communication with the ship above, so I had no other choice but to wait out the storm.

Even with old-fashioned radio waves, losing communication wasn't common. The winds must have had something unique in their makeup to cause the interference.

I waited for a tad less than five minutes before I heard something through the radio. "This is the captain. Do you read me, Commander?"

"I read you loud and clear, Captain," I answered.

"Good," he replied. "I'm sorry about the storm. It came in just as the lander detached, and Vanessa couldn't predict it when you were still on board."

"I'm sorry, Erma!" I heard Vanessa shout.

"It's fine. I'm still alive. I just feel bad for the one that's going to clean up the lander."

"Good, your sense of humor is still intact," the captain transmitted. "The storm has passed, by the way, so you can descend into the tunnels whenever you're ready."

"I'm on it," I said, and opened the hatch again. I exited the lander and walked towards the rover, covered in a layer of brown dirt, that stood a couple of meters away. I went to the front of it, grabbed a cable, and attached it to my vessel.

I walked towards the hole that had been drilled, stood by the edge of it for at least ten seconds, and stared into the pitch-blackness that was its center.

"I can still come down and join you if you want," I heard the captain say. "I understand if you don't think this is a one-person job."

He surprised me. How did he know I was having second thoughts? And then I realized. The rover I was standing in front of had cameras installed on the bumper and was transmitting a live feed of me to Vanessa.

I felt ashamed. I didn't want them to know I feared entering the hole, not after I acted all tough when I was on the ship.

"Not a one-person job? How about not a three-person job?" I snarked, trying to hide my embarrassment.

I sighed and looked at the camera of the rover. "It's fine," I continued. "I can do this. I'll call you when I need help."

"Alright," the captain said. "Go get 'em." And then I saw two flashes from the headlights of the rover.

I turned around and faced the hole again. I climbed down and then lowered myself further into it by using the rover. Three meters in and I activated my night vision so I could see the ground, but it was no use. I still couldn't see the end of the hole, just the pitch-black center.

I could see my arms—which were both holding onto the cable—trembling. Stupid engineers. The trembling was just another useless feature added to make us feel more human. It wasn't helping in this situation; it only made it worse.

The more I lowered myself into the hole, the more the circle of light on top shrank.

"Captain?" I asked, my words echoing around me in the hole.

No response.

I had lowered myself less than a hundred meters into this hole and already had I lost communication. Whatever the planet's outer layer was made out of it didn't seem to allow radio waves to pass through.

I noticed the transition from the rocky surface to the metallic tunnel and wanted to take a sample of it, but I didn't have the tools to do so. I assumed Wendy already took a sample, so I didn't worry too much. I did have to find her first, though.

After a couple of minutes of descending into the hole—and almost into a panic attack—I had finally reached the ground, noticeably covered with dirt. I looked around and saw the tracks of the others—lightly faded now, most likely due to that little storm. The tracks led into one of the two tunnels, but it was closed off by a wall. I suppose I had found the reason the others hadn't come back up.

I released the cable attached to me and approached the wall. Immediately, I noticed an interference with my magnetometer which got stronger the closer to the wall I walked. They must've followed this interference.

I proceeded to knock on the wall to try and estimate how thick it actually was. The muted, dull sound generated by my knocking cleared up why there was no evidence of Wendy using her plasma lance to cut through it. It was just too thick.

I grabbed the cable I had just thrown on the ground, and quickly attached it to myself again. I raised myself all the way to the surface so I could ask the captain to send down the one thing I had never used—but had so badly wanted to—in all of my two thousand years as a cognioid.

"Captain?" I called over the radio the moment I reached the surface.

"That was fast," said the captain. "Were the others just laying at the bottom of the tunnel?"

"No, I haven't found them yet."

"Oh, then why did you come back up?"

"The tunnel splits into two down there. One of the branches is closed off by a wall, and I'm a hundred percent sure the others went through there."

"Wait," he said abruptly. "Do you think that wall fell

down after they walked through that tunnel?"

"Yes."

"Fuck," he said, sighing deeply. "Vanessa."

"Yes, Captain?" Vanessa asked.

"You can send that message pod now."

"On it."

"And you said a hundred percent sure that they went through there?" he clarified. "How are you so certain?"

"Well, firstly, there's an anomaly behind that wall that is messing up my magnetometer. Secondly—and this was the dead giveaway—their tracks lead into that tunnel."

"What do you mean by messing up your magnetometer?"

"It's hard to explain. It causes it to go all over the place. I won't be able to use it to navigate through the tunnels."

"Alright. So, what's the plan?"

"Well, we need to get through that wall," I said. "And I was thinking that maybe we could use the—"

"Stop," he said, cutting me off. "Are you sure there's no other way?"

"There is another tunnel that goes into the opposite direction. Maybe I should go in there and never find them?" I said sarcastically.

"I'm sending the vanishers now," he added, without asking any more questions.

I grinned cheerfully, pumping my fists, and literally jumping for joy. I had never been more excited in my entire life. Mining this planet was a great idea!

I couldn't wait to use the vanishers. They were an extremely unique form of weaponry, and it was one of the latest inventions delivered by our engineers, completely state of the art. They used a miniscule amount of exotic matter as their source of energy, and, when triggered, caused a one-of-a-kind adjustable *implosion*, instead of the traditional fixed explosion. I had never seen it used in real life, only in videos and in virtual simulations.

Having the ability to generate a controlled implosion had several benefits, the most important one was that there was no destructive effect on the surroundings, only on the area intended to be removed. With a deviation of less than five centimeters, it was like a very precise eraser of our reality. But the best part? The implosion looked amazing, or at least that's what I'd seen in the videos and simulations.

I walked to the rover and leaned against it, the cable still attached to my vessel. While waiting for the vanisher to be sent down, I zoomed in on the part of the red-colored sky where Vanessa's vessel should've been, and sure enough, after a couple of seconds of searching, I could see her drifting.

A small little dot detached from her vessel; a supply pod, containing the Vanishers. The supply pod was basically like a lander, but a lot smaller. Like the scouters, they were single use only. It wasn't as wasteful and environmentally unfriendly as it seemed. Both the scouters and the supply pods were biodegradable and cheap to make.

I saw the supply pod entering the atmosphere, creating a bright orange fireball against the red sky. As it came closer, the fire dissipated and I could see its white coloring, with some black scorching on the bottom. As it was about to land, four stabilizing boosters beneath the pod slowed it down, and safely delivered it a hundred meters from my location.

"Couldn't let it land closer to me, could you?" I asked.

"Sorry, but I didn't want to risk that thing hitting you," the captain said. "Then I'd have to go into the tunnel."

"Very funny," I said.

I proceeded to release the cable that was still attached to my vessel walked over the supply pod.

When I reached the pod, I saw that its bottom half was completely scorched black and there was smoke all around it. It had no handles to open it, and no buttons either, just a very thin line at the middle where the two small hatches of it met. I wirelessly connected to it, and sent a signal to open it, but the little screen on the top right corner flashed red, with a message that said: UNAUTHORIZED ACCESS.

"Something is wrong," I radioed to the ship. "It won't let me open it, and it gives me a message that says, 'unauthorized access'."

"Oh!" I heard the captain shout. "I'm sorry, I forgot to give you clearance."

I couldn't help but feel offended at that. I was the commander of the ship, sacrificing myself to save my crewmembers, and I still wasn't important enough to be given access to the vanishers?

"Okay, that should do it," the captain continued. "Try opening it again."

I sent another signal and, sure enough, the screen flashed green, followed by a message that read: ACCESS GRANTED TO ERMA VAN HOUT.

The two hatches slowly hissed open, revealing the contents inside. I grinned again but tried to hide it in case there was another camera somewhere I didn't know about.

Two oval-shaped vanishers the size of apples, dark gray in color, were placed neatly in the center of the container. Each had enough power to delete objects the size of mountains, and *I* was going to get to use it on a measly metal wall. I couldn't hide my excitement and grinned uncontrollably. It was kind of evil of me to trick my captain into using them, but I didn't care, because what I was about to do was worth manipulating my superiors.

I grabbed both vanishers, which had a gel-like consistency, connected to both of them wirelessly, and placed them in the compartment in my chest. No amount of force or beating would be able to trigger them, not even if I smashed it with a hammer. All it needed was my encrypted signal.

I walked back to the rover, attached the cable to my vessel again, and lowered myself into the hole and all the way to the ground. This time not with fear, but with excitement.

I detached the cable from my vessel, approached the thick metal wall, opened the compartment in my chest, and took out one of the vanishers.

It felt like I was grabbing a rubbery ball. I pushed it on the exact center of the wall and sent a command to make the side of the vanisher against the wall adhesive. I let go of it and was giddy when I saw it had worked. I then tried to move the vanisher around the wall—up, down, every direction possible—with as much force as I could generate, but it still stuck firmly to the center of the wall.

I walked backwards past the hole I had entered through and a couple meters into the opposite tunnel. My night vision was on, so I wouldn't be able to see the implosion in color, but it didn't matter to me. I was still going to see it. From where I stood safely out of range, I programmed it to implode with a diameter of two meters, which was more than enough for me to walk through the wall, and then I sent the signal for it to detonate.

Just as happened in the hyperdrive, I could see the matter around it warping and swirling into the vanisher with a quiet zapping sound. Within two seconds, a hole appeared in the thick metal wall.

Chapter 22
Finding Bobby

I stepped through the hole. The metal wall was at least half a meter thick, but when I reached the other side of it, I immediately noticed something strange. The atmosphere was different, and it was slowly changing to mimic atmosphere on the surface now that I had made a hole connecting both sides.

I didn't think too much about the atmosphere. My vessel recorded everything, so I could give the data to the ROCAL to analyze and they could worry about it. What mattered to me most was finding the others and getting the mind chips.

I lucked out that the ground was covered in dirt and that all I had to do was to follow the tracks, finding the others was going to be a lot easier than expected.

There was a tunnel that branched off from the one I was in, but I didn't think too much about that either.

The tunnels after the bifurcation were beautiful. There were inscriptions on the walls that added a bit of mystery to the place. The writing didn't match anything from the database that I had uploaded into me, which indicated that the inscriptions couldn't have been made by humans. I was happy to know that the captain had sent a message pod because this was most definitely not the result of a natural phenomenon.

I continued following the tracks, in the direction of the magnetic disturbance, all the way to a strange-looking door. It was locked and there didn't seem to be any way to unlock it. There was no button, no keyhole, not even handles.

There had to be a way to get to the other side. The tracks led right through this door, which meant the others had found a way to unlock it.

I searched the surrounding walls but couldn't find anything that was obviously meant to unlock this door. That was until I stepped back and saw an odd bump with two holes on the right wall. I walked closer to examine it, put two fingers in the holes, and realized quickly it was a rotating mechanism.

When I rotated it completely clockwise, I looked at the door to see if opening it had been as simple as that. Luckily, it was.

I opened the door completely and was awestruck at what I saw.

There was a tall structure with a sphere in the middle of it standing in the room. That definitely had to be the source of the magnetic disturbance because my magnetometer was going all over the place.

As I had done in the branched tunnel, I ignored the structure and followed the prints; they led to another door across the room, so that's where I went. Just as I was about to go through it, the other door slammed shut, causing me to jump.

I walked back to the first door and pushed on it, but it was locked. Luckily, there was another one of those rotating bumps on the wall. I did the same thing as I had done with the first bump and rotated it clockwise. Sure enough, it unlocked the door, which gave me a great sense of relief. I was starting to think I was going to be trapped in here.

I proceeded to follow the tracks once more into the door across the first one, and that's when I realized something different about the atmosphere. It had water.

In many cases, water in the atmosphere was a good thing, but I had hoped not to find water in the atmosphere in these tunnels. Water could only mean one thing. Life.

But that wasn't the worst part. When I passed through the door, I noticed something very odd on the ground. Jumbled between the tracks of the cognioids was another set of tracks in a very unorthodox pattern.

This can't be happening! Is there really something alive down here?

A quick shiver coursed through my vessel, as if I was getting goosebumps—another useless feature added by our engineers. I really couldn't imagine what Bobby went through when he experienced all of this, especially considering he wasn't backed up.

Shaking off my uneasiness, I continued on. The tunnel I was in now was different than the other one. This tunnel was wider, taller, and had different inscriptions.

I finally reached a door after a couple of minutes of walking. Thankfully, this one was unlocked.

I slowly pushed it open and looked through the opening, but there was nothing behind the door. Just a room with four other doors along one wall.

There seemed to be a dried-up substance on the floor that trailed through the fourth door, along with those unorthodox tracks. I disabled my night vision and turned on my flashlight to get a better look. The substance on the ground was purple.

The dirt on the ground was scuffed, and there were tracks going in every direction. The tracks from the cognioids went through the first door on the left, but then another set of cognioid tracks appeared from the second door and went back through the first again, but that wasn't everything. There seemed to be two tracks coming from the first door and going into the third. One set of tracks belonged to a cognioid, and the other set belonged to whatever else was down here.

I had no clue of what had happened here and the evidence around me didn't help to clarify anything.

I decided to go into the first door, seeing as it was the

one where most tracks went in and out of.

I approached the door tentatively and slowly opened it, cautiously peering through the opening. If I had a stomach, what I saw would have made it drop.

It was Bobby.

His vessel was cut in half, most likely by the thick metal wall behind him.

I ran towards him, grabbed him by the shoulders, and shook him furiously.

“Bobby!” I shouted. “Bobby!”

No response.

His battery must’ve malfunctioned. Now that I was closer, I could see that a part of the battery had been destroyed by the wall. But I wasn’t worried. I had expected him to be powered down by now anyway. Still, I felt bad for him.

I shook my head. I had come down here for one thing. I immediately grabbed his head with both my hands, turned it a hundred and eighty degrees, and removed it so I could recover his mind chip.

Part VI

Lester Pierce

The Captain

Chapter 23

A Joint Effort

Standing behind the side window of the bridge, looking down on the fecal-colored planet, I wondered if I had made the right decision, waiting so long before sending a message pod.

There wasn't any concrete evidence that the tunnel was artificial *before* Erma told me about that wall, *and* the scouters couldn't be trusted. At least that's what I kept telling myself so I didn't feel as guilty.

But even if the tunnels were artificial, the rest of the crew would still be okay, right? They were cognioids for crying out loud.

And Bobby not being backed up wasn't that big of a problem either, we could still recover his mind chip, unless something happened to his head, which I highly doubted. Aluminum was still considered a strong substance.

The worst and most probable thing that could occur was that there were booby traps down there, like that wall Erma had mentioned.

I hoped that Erma was going to succeed recovering everyone's chips, so we could get the heck out of here and leave the rest for the ROCAL.

I shook my head, disappointed in myself.

"What are you thinking about?" I heard Vanessa say.

I turned around, walked to my favorite chair by the table and sank into it. "Nothing," I replied. "Just waiting for the commander."

I picked up my book that was resting on the table and looked at it from every angle. What a useless piece of junk.

It was a book on how to colonize planetary systems the right way, but the guy who wrote it had since been highly discredited. He stated in one chapter that if humankind didn't have hyperdrives or cryo-pods, they could send machines and human embryos.

The machines would build the base, terraform the planet, and, when everything was ready, incubate the embryos. This was utter nonsense.

The right way would be to send only the machines and let them do everything. That's how humanity did it in the past and it worked for us. It would be a waste of time and energy to care for the embryos anyway.

"It was a good choice to send the message pod," Vanessa said, bringing me out of my internal literary criticism.

"Let's hope it wasn't too late."

"I'm sure it wasn't. It's only been forty-eight hours."

I shrugged after she said that and pretended to read the book.

She was trying to make me feel better, which was surprising considering we had had a heated argument earlier about sending the pod in the first place.

Despite her attempts at reassurance, I knew she was wrong. And I knew that she knew that too. *A lot* can happen in forty-eight hours; she was just being the gold-hearted ship she always has been. A quality about her that I admired and was envious of.

As a captain, you sometimes have to make hard decisions and you can't let your emotions factor into them. That's where protocols came in handy, but our situation wasn't represented in *any* of the protocols we had uploaded so I was at a bit of a loss. Had I actually made a decision out of fear? Were Vanessa and Erma right about me?

The message pod was going to take at least an hour before it would reach the ROCAL, and it would take another two hours for them and the military to come to our location. We sent them all the data collected from the planet—including parts of the tunnels—and mentioned the fact that there was a trap wall in there, just so they would take us more seriously.

"I know you're not reading, Captain," Vanessa continued, trying to coax me into conversation.

"What?"

"Your eyes aren't moving a single nanometer, and they aren't focused on the book."

"I'm practicing mindfulness."

She sighed deeply. "Talk to me, Captain. Please!"

Her holographic image dropped to her knees to emphasize her plea for a conversation with me.

"Waiting for the commander is torture," she continued.

"Okay, okay," I said, trying to calm her down. "Let's talk, but only under one condition."

"What is it?"

"Promise me you won't ever beg for anything again."

"I was just trying to be dramatic, but alright, I promise."

I chuckled lightly. "So, what do you want to talk about?"

"Well, off the top of my head, what do you think will happen to us if there really are aliens down there?"

"Not entirely sure. We may become famous, but I don't think I'd like that."

"Why not?"

"I like to live my life in peace and discretion, and not have strangers poke their noses into it."

"You could monetize that fame though."

"I am content with what I have."

"Don't you have a purpose you always wanted to fulfill but didn't have enough credits for?"

I sat silently in my chair, trying hard to think of an answer.

"I never thought about it," I answered.

"What are you passionate about then?"

"Following protocol, I suppose. I do like hierarchies though."

"So, you want to move up the ladder. Is that it? Because being famous will definitely help with that."

"No, not that. I just like how a system or governing body is built. Without it, everything would go to shit."

"Huh," she said, with a surprised tone in her voice, as if she had been expecting a completely different answer.

"What about you?" I asked. "Do you want to become famous?"

Her hologram gave a little shrug. "Wouldn't hurt I suppose. I could use—"

But before Vanessa could finish her sentence, Erma's voice crackled through the radio.

"Captain! Come in. Captain!"

"I'm here!" I shouted back as I quickly got up and ran to the monitor displaying the rover's camera feed. "Give me some good news, Commander."

I saw through the camera that she was climbing out of the hole she had lowered herself into roughly an hour ago. She didn't have a single scratch on her vessel which gave me a colossal sense of relief.

"It's Bobby! H-His vessel…it's been damaged by a wall."

"Fuck."

"That's not all."

"What do you mean?"

"His head, Captain. I-It's been pried open."

"What do you mean pried open?"

"I think someone, or something, tried to get his chip."

"Oh my god!" I heard Vanessa wail.

"Please tell me it's still there," I continued.

"It's gone. Whatever wanted it has it."

That's when I couldn't hold it in anymore. I swung my fist forward, putting a hole through the monitor that displayed Erma.

I leaned forward, head sunken down, and rested my arms on the control panels that were in front of me.

"Did you find the others?" I asked.

"No, just Bobby, but…" she paused for a moment then said, "there's more."

"What?"

"The tunnels have inscriptions on them. There are also doors everywhere, and a weird metal object that messes with my magnetometer."

"The ROCAL will handle that."

"I'm not finished, Captain."

I shook my head slowly, frustrated. "What else is there?"

"I saw strange tracks, definitely not of a cognioid, and a purple substance on the floor. I think it might be the blood of whatever is living down there, Captain."

"Good," I said. "At least we know it bleeds." I pushed myself off of the control panels, gathered myself, and walked towards the corridor of the bridge.

"Where are you going?" Vanessa asked.

"To get a weapon. I'm going down there to get our crew back. Commander, stay put. I'm joining you."

It was a good thing I had charged up while the commander was in her hibernation station.

"Do I really have to go in there again?" Erma asked hesitantly. "Telling you about Bobby isn't the only reason I came back up."

"I understand if you're having second thoughts, but two cognioids going down there is better than one."

"But what if the same thing that happened to Bobby happens to me? We have the same type of frame."

"I can't promise that nothing will happen to you, but it's a risk you'll have to take. The crew needs us, Commander."

She didn't say anything with my reminder of why we needed to go down there. Since I'd destroyed the monitor, I couldn't see her, but I knew she was weighing her options.

A couple seconds of silence passed.

"Okay," I heard her say. "Let's do this. Just don't let my chip fall into the hands of whatever is down there."

"I'll do my best."

I was already in the arsenal grabbing a plasma cannon and fixing it onto one of my shoulders.

I got into one of the landers, entered the coordinates, and blasted off into the planet's atmosphere. The planet that sprouted so many questions I still didn't have answers to. The planet that looked like it came out of a horse's behind. The planet that might harbor the only evidence of life other than our own. The planet that was going to change the course of humanity. The oddest fucking planet I'd ever come across.

Chapter 24

Biting the Dust

I landed fifty meters from the hole they had drilled and when I crawled out of the lander the first thing I noticed was the discrepancy between the sky and the ground. The ground was a darkish brown, and the sky was bloodred with a tint of pink—scary to see, but intriguing to think about.

I walked towards the commander, who was sitting on the ground next to the rover, shoulders sunken, head down. She looked as if she was considering ending her life to avoid going into the tunnels with me.

"Are you okay?" I asked when I got to her.

"Let's just do this."

"Alright. Don't worry; even if we fail, the ROCAL and the military will be here in less than three hours."

"What if whatever is underneath already did something with Bobby's chip by then? There is valuable information on that chip, Captain."

"I know. That's why we're going down there right now to get those chips back before it's too late."

She sighed deeply and pushed herself off the ground, stood up straight, and put her shoulders back.

"Vanessa?" she said. "I'm uploading the footage of the inscriptions on the walls I recorded to you right now. See if you can match the inscriptions to anything in your database."

"Just got it," Vanessa replied after a second. "I'm analyzing it now."

"Good."

Erma walked towards the hole with the cable from the rover attached to her vessel. When she reached the edge of the hole, she turned around, staring at me since I hadn't moved. "Are we going to do this or what?" she asked.

I nodded, grabbed a cable from the rover, and attached it to my vessel. I followed her all the way to the bottom of the hole where I saw everything she had described earlier. The dirt on the ground with the weird tracks, the inscriptions on the walls, the mysterious metal tower that affect the magnetometers. I didn't waste any energy thinking about these things. All I wanted was to recover the mind chips of our crew.

We eventually got to Bobby's vessel, which was just laying face down in the dirt, crushed in half by a metal wall, one that looked similar to the one Erma had put a hole through with a vanisher.

"Let's not waste any time here," I said, without touching Bobby's mangled vessel.

"This is as far as I had gone before I made my way back to the surface. I think you should take the lead from here on."

She was scared, and so was I. But I couldn't show my fear; I couldn't let her know that her captain was dreaded by the same tunnels he had forced her into. My only option was to agree.

"Our best bet is the third door," I said.

"I think so too."

It was the most logical option, because two sets of tracks led from Bobby to there; one from a cognioid, and one from whatever else was down here. That meant that one of the crew was either held captive, or that one of the crew was following whatever took Bobby's chip. It couldn't be that a cognioid took the chip and was followed, because the way Bobby's head was pried open didn't reflect the actions of a cognioid. A cognioid would have manually ejected it.

We walked an agonizing fifteen hundred meters in

that tunnel, every meter increasing my worry over what we were about to experience. We didn't utter a single word during our trek through the tunnel, not until we reached the end where we encountered another door.

"Stay behind me, I'll go check it out," I said.

"Oh, don't worry. I wasn't planning on getting in front of you."

I rolled my eyes at her, but I understood what had prompted her comment. An alien life form that knows the importance of our mind chips was enough for anyone to abandon this planet and annihilate it, the same as we had done with most parasites in the past.

I crept up to the door, trying not to make a single sound as I opened it and looked inside.

"It's Nate!" I screamed, opening the door in one fast swing. Erma quickly followed me as I ran into the small room towards Nate's powered-down vessel.

He was laying faceup with his plasma cannon on his shoulder and a plasma ray in each of his hands.

I stood over his vessel.

Erma was standing behind me, looking over my shoulder, focused on Nate's head. Her curiosity led me to believe that we had the same question in mind.

I quickly turned his vessel over so we could see the back of his head.

"Dear God. Not him too!" Erma cried.

It was gone. His mind chip was gone. His head had been pried open in the same manner as Bobby's.

I let go, dropping Nate on the ground. Although I guess it wasn't Nate anymore; it was just an empty vessel, with Nate's signature tribal markings and a mutilated head.

"What now?" Erma asked.

"I suppose the next thing to do is for me to apologize to you."

"What do you mean?"

"It's all my fault."

"No, don't say that."

"Argh!" I screamed and dropped to my knees, looking over Nate's empty vessel. "If I had sent a message pod earlier, they might have been saved by now."

"None of us knew what was going on here," Erma said, trying to console me.

I sighed and got back on my feet. But as I was getting up, I noticed a something strange next to Nate's vessel. I picked it up.

"What is it?" Erma asked.

"Oh no."

"What? Let me see!" she demanded.

I turned my vessel around, showing it to her.

She gasped loudly.

"He didn't. He couldn't have!" she wailed.

I looked around the room, and sure enough, a meter away, there was another one. I pointed my finger towards it, showing it to Erma. There was no doubt about it. These were the shattered pieces of Bobby's and Wendy's mind chips.

"YOU ASSHOLE!" Erma screamed as she pushed me out of the way and started to pound on Nate's vessel, scratching parts of the tribal prints off of his body plates.

I immediately grabbed her and stopped her from doing any more damage. I could feel her trembling in my arms—a stupid feature left in by our engineers.

"It's okay, Erma. It's okay."

"No, it's not! He killed Bobby!"

"I know but think about why he did it. This way they won't get their hands on the chips."

Her crying made me feel weak in every part of my vessel, even if she couldn't produce any tears.

"Then why didn't he shoot himself as well? Why did he leave his own chip for them to take!? It doesn't make any sense!"

She was right, it didn't make sense. His chip was just as valuable as the others, if he destroyed Wendy's and

Bobby's mind chips to prevent them from getting into the wrong hands, the next logical step would be to destroy his own.

I know the lieutenant didn't have the best personality, he'd always get in trouble with the rest of the crew, but he would never kill someone for no reason. That I was sure of.

"We need to find his chip," I said.

"No! I'm going back up. I'm not going to risk my life to save that murderer's chip."

"We still don't know everything yet, Commander. For all we know, the things living down here got to his chip before he could destroy it."

She stood silent for a moment, thinking about what I had said. "Fine!" She got up on her feet. "But I get to interrogate that asshole when we've recovered his chip."

"As you wish."

The next thing I did was reach for the lieutenant's bag to see what was in it.

One plasma cannon.

"Hey. How many plasma cannons and plasma rays did the lieutenant bring down again?" I asked.

"Three of each. Why?"

"There seems to be one of each missing."

"Do you think they—"

"It's likely," I said abruptly.

"Do we have to recover those as well?"

"Our first priority is the mind chips. They contain much more valuable information. If we have time, we can look for the weapons as well."

What a nightmare. Whatever was living down here knew what it was doing and what it wanted. It understood what was important. It was intelligent to a point that was mortifying.

Chapter 25

Octagonal Twin

I took the weapons from Kendrick and put them in my own bag, then I opened the compartment in his chest. In there were four of Wendy's sample containers.

"Are they empty?" Erma asked.

I grabbed one of the containers and inspected it. "No," I answered, and showed her the little red indicator that signified it had a sample inside. I proceeded to take all four containers and put them into the compartment of my own chest. "We need to keep moving."

I approached the door across the room, Erma following behind. Whatever took Nate's chip must've gone through there. There didn't seem to be any tracks that went the other way, at least not any fresh ones.

"What is that?" she asked, pointing to a weird device on the wall next to the door.

"Not sure, but it seems to have been tampered with."

"Do you think the lieutenant did that?"

"I don't know. It's not important. We just need to find his chip and get the heck out of here."

I moved swiftly to the door and peered through cautiously.

It was an octagonal room, clear of any sign of life. There were four rows of what looked like rectangular metal blocks, I couldn't tell what they were exactly because, just like the rest of the tunnels, it was completely dark in the room and my night vision could only see so much.

Across the room was another door with the same weird device next to it, which also appeared to have been tampered with. At least that's what it looked from the distance I was at.

I signaled Erma it was safe to enter and we strolled in to investigate.

"They look like—"

"Computers," I finished her sentence.

"They have fucking computers?"

"Apparently."

"But they're destroyed."

"I think the lieutenant did that. His tracks are all around this place," I pointed towards the ground, showing her the lieutenant's tracks. That's when I noticed puddles of a dried-up substance.

I turned on my flashlight and deactivated my night vision to see what color the substance was. Dark purple, just like the one from before.

"He sure put up a fight," I continued.

"But there aren't any bodies here, so I don't think he killed them."

"Or somebody cleaned up the bodies before we got here."

I turned my attention to the computers.

"The screens are like a flap; you can open them," I said, as I played with the openable screens.

"What's inside?"

"Nothing, just some components on the sides, and a little platform in the middle. I think it's a scanner of some sort."

"I think I know what happened here."

"What?"

"I think Nate found Bobby's vessel just like we did and followed the tracks all the way to this room. He must've seen them scanning it in one of these computers, so he shot every one of the aliens, and destroyed the computers."

"That doesn't explain why he's laying out there without his mind chip."

"Maybe there were too many of them, and they got to him as he was running away."

"Perhaps. We need to find him, that way we'll know what really happened."

I turned off my flashlight and reactivated my night vision.

I approached the next door, and what I saw through this one astonished me.

Six tall, skinny creatures, with two eyes as big as apples. They had a freakishly tiny mouth which could at most fit a pencil. Four limbs, two upper and two lower, with what appeared to be claws at the end of the upper ones, and at the end of those claws little stubs.

They looked peculiarly humanoid, yet unhuman.

I stood still behind the door, frozen, unable to even whisper a single word.

"What do you see?" Erma asked.

I couldn't answer; I was still in shock over what was behind the door.

"Captain?" she continued.

I shook my head, and whispered, "Six aliens, two of them armed."

"Fuck," I heard Erma whisper back.

They were in another octagonal room with the same four rows of computers, but these ones weren't destroyed. The screens were lit up, and so were the buttons and dials that four of the creatures were using. The two others were patrolling the room, with what I assumed were weapons.

This was the end of our road. There was no door on the other side of this room. Nate's mind chip *had* to be in this room, behind one of those screens, if my assessment of their function had been correct.

"Ready your weapon, Commander," I whispered.

"What's the plan?"

"We need to be careful with these beings. They managed to destroy two of our crew members' vessels. We have no idea what else they're capable of."

"Be careful huh?" Erma repeated. "You think I don't know that?"

"I wasn't done."

"Sorry, continue."

"I say we storm in and shoot them as fast as possible, the armed ones first, before they can retaliate."

"Okay, good. What if they have shields?"

"I don't see any shields, so we're safe."

She nodded.

"Okay, ready?" I asked.

"Ready."

I started to count down from three, and when I hit zero, I slammed my shoulder into the door, causing it to swing open. I ran into the room and started to shoot at the armed creatures. Erma was right behind me, doing the same.

The creatures quickly turned to face us, not making a single sound. I saw one of my charges going straight towards one of the armed creatures, but it was deflected by an invisible force.

"Shields!" I screamed.

The creatures fired back, releasing white pulses of energy that were accompanied by zooming sounds. The creatures behind the computers ran towards the ones with weapons, taking cover behind them.

I grabbed Erma and pulled her behind one of the rectangular computers.

"You said they didn't have shields!" Erma screamed at me.

"They're invisible! How was I supposed to know?"

"What now!?"

"I'm thinking! Just keep shooting at them so they won't come our way."

We kept firing with our cannons over the row of alien

computers, and I could hear zooming sounds behind us hitting the computers. Luckily for us, the row of computers we had our backs against deflected whatever came out of their weapons, or so I thought.

"I know what to do!" Erma shouted. She opened her chest compartment and took out an oval-shaped device. A massive smile spread across my face.

"I love you!" I screamed joyfully.

But just as she was about to throw it, a pulse of white energy penetrated the row of computers and hit her right between the eyes.

"Erma!" I screamed, as I saw her drop to the ground letting go of the vanisher, which subsequently rolled underneath the row of computers.

"Fuck!" I yelled out over the zooming sounds zapping against the computers.

I quickly turned her over.

She was gone. The blast had gone right through her mind chip.

I bolted from the room away from these creatures.

I ran through the other octagonal room and into the room where Nate's vessel lay. I stopped and pressed my back against the door, pushing it with all my strength, hoping they wouldn't barge in and do the same to me as they had done to Erma.

I had never experienced this much angst in my entire life. They had one-shotted Erma and I had no idea how my steel frame would fare against their weapons.

Nate's vessel was laying two meters in front of me, reminding me what could become of me if I stayed in these tunnels any longer.

I tried to think of a plan. I had to come up with something. I was the captain for crying out loud.

That's when I noticed the reading on my atmospheric analyzer, and it hit me.

I knew exactly what I had to do.

Chapter 26

The Captain's Plan

I calculated the distance between me and the creatures I knew were behind me. A hundred and fifty meters. I ran the other way, counting every meter. I couldn't use my magnetometer because of the interference, so I remembered every degree of angle I took at every turn.

After fifteen hundred meters, I reached the big room with five doors, one behind which Bobby's vessel laid. I turned again, remembering how many degrees it was, and ran past the mysterious structure where I unlocked the door that guarded it, using the method Erma had shown me when she led me to Bobby.

I eventually got to the hole we had come in through, attached the cable to my vessel, and raised myself up to the surface as fast as I possibly could, dying to get my message to Vanessa.

"Vanessa!" I yelled, as I climbed out of the hole.

"Yes, Captain?"

"Order one of the miners to this location," I said as I stood facing the direction of the room with five doors. "Fourteen hundred and fifty meters in the direction I'm facing."

"Got it."

"From that point, turn eighty degrees to the right, and go sixteen hundred and fifty meters. Land it there."

"I've sent the instructions."

"One last thing: can you check from the scouter's data if there's an octagonal-shaped cavity beneath that location? There should be two octagons next to one another.

I want it to land on top of the one that has no tunnels connected to it."

"There's nothing there, according to the scouters."

"Fuck, it might be too deep."

"Do you want me to cancel the order?"

"No, we just have to gamble, I guess."

"Alright, miner number three has the instructions."

The nearest miner, a hundred meters away, the one that had drilled the entrance, lifted off the ground and flew towards the location I had given Vanessa.

"Where is the commander?" she asked

"She's gone. They shot her."

"Fuck!" I heard her yell through the radio. It was the first time I had ever heard her swear.

"It's fine, she has a backup,"

"I know, but still. What about the others?"

"Wendy's and Bobby's chips are destroyed. I think the lieutenant's is beneath the location I just sent you."

"But Bobby—"

"I know," I quickly interrupted her. "Just… just don't."

"Oh my god. Bobby…"

"When the miner has landed, instruct it to drill until it reaches a hollow space."

"Okay…"

I uncoupled the cable from my vessel and ran towards the rover, but I suddenly realized something and stopped.

"Hey, I'm uploading you the footage from below so you can analyze it."

"Okay."

With the footage sent to Vanessa, I proceeded to run towards one of the landers.

"And I'm sending you some samples in one of the landers, can you analyze those too?"

"I'll send one of the AIs to pick it up once it's gotten

to the ship."

"Great."

I got to the lander and put the four containers in it, then wirelessly transmitted an instruction. It closed its hatch and lifted off the ground, blasting towards Vanessa.

I ran back to the rover and got in. I instructed it to retract every cable back to its front and drive to the same location I had sent the miner.

The ride was a bumpy one due to the extremely uneven surface of the planet, but I eventually reached the miner, which had just started drilling into the ground.

I got out of the rover, and leaned up against it with my arms crossed, patiently waiting for the warning the miner was going to give when it reached a hollow area.

"I'm done analyzing the footage the commander had sent me," Vanessa radioed to me.

"Great, anything interesting?"

"No, the writing doesn't match anything from my database, and I have a complete copy of the biggest database known to mankind."

"It was expected, I suppose. What about the footage I just uploaded?"

"Still analyzing."

"And the samples?"

"Just got them into the lab; haven't started yet."

"Alright."

I waited another five minutes before the miner gave its warning and stopped drilling.

"You can move the miner now," I radioed to Vanessa.

She didn't reply, but she had clearly heard me because the miner launched upwards and landed a couple meters away.

I waited another ten minutes, enough time for the atmosphere from the surface to travel to the octagonal room below, hopefully suffocating the creatures that destroyed

Erma's chip, or at least drive them away.

When the ten minutes passed, I took a cable from the rover and attached it to my vessel again, lowering myself into the new hole that had been drilled. This time, I lowered myself very slowly, ready to pull myself back up in an instant if something was still lurking down there.

As I was lowering myself down, a thought came to mind. What if they take Nate's chip elsewhere? It was a possibility, especially if they were as intelligent as I thought they were. I just had to hope for the best.

Eventually, I could see the bottom of the hole with my night vision.

I stopped before I reached the inside of the room, dangling above it in the drilled opening. I lowered myself little by little, so I could see the inside of the room.

Nothing.

The creatures were gone.

The hole was almost in the exact center of the room. I could see Erma's vessel laying behind the row of computers where we had taken cover.

I lowered myself completely to the ground. The screens of the computers were still on, except the ones that the creatures had shot.

Despite being inside the room, I didn't detach the cable from my vessel. The creatures could storm into the room at any moment.

I walked past every computer screen, starting from the one that was shot at, and opening each of them as I walked by them.

The first, empty.

The second, also empty.

But by the third one, I had found it. Nate's mind chip, unscathed.

I quickly opened my chest compartment and placed it neatly inside before raising myself back up towards the hole.

But two meters above the ground I realized I had forgotten something. I readied my cannon, aimed at my target, and shot at every computer, destroying them until they looked just like the ones in the next room.

When I reached the surface, I radioed Vanessa, "Pack everything up and let's get the heck out of here. I've got Nate's chip."

"Great!" I heard her shout in a joyful tone.

Driving all the way back to one of the landers, a grin was plastered on my face the whole journey. It was finally over.

Putting one foot into the lander, I turned back and gazed at edges of the craters on the horizon. The dirty brown color of the soil, the dead, unbreathable atmosphere that breezed in every direction, and the bloodred sky with a pink tint. I'd shed a tear if I were human, knowing how much my crew suffered on this planet. A planet we weren't supposed to be on in the first place; a planet that looked despicable from the outside, and yet was the home of not just alien life, but intelligent alien life.

"A very odd planet, indeed," I murmured.

Chapter 27

The Results

When I got to the ship, the first thing I did was walk to the bridge and insert Nate's chip into one of the slots. It loaded in less than a second, and immediately I heard, "Argh!"

I stepped back in surprise.

"You scared me there, Lieutenant," I said.

"W-W-Where am I!?" he muttered loudly.

"It's okay, you can relax now. You're back on the ship."

At that point, he started to do the one thing I had never expected him to do, not from the fierce, and sometimes arrogant cognioid that was Nate Kendrick.

He started to cry.

Just as when Erma was crying near his mindless vessel, I felt weak. I had no idea what to say.

"It's okay," Vanessa said to him. "We can go home now."

"I-I'm so sorry," he sobbed. "I had no choice but to destroy their chips. I had no choice but to kill Bobby."

"What!?" Vanessa shouted.

I raised my hands at Vanessa, signaling her not to continue with the barrage of questions I was sure she had.

"Watch the footage I sent you, it's all in there," I told her. I then turned my attention back to the lieutenant. "It's alright, I understand why you did it."

"I-I tried to shoot my own chip, but my battery ran out."

That answered Erma's question. Which meant her assault of his vessel hadn't been justified.

"Can I please delete all of this from my memory?" he continued to sob.

"We still need to be debriefed. After that, you can do as you wish."

He didn't utter a single word after that, instead remaining completely silent.

"Captain," Vanessa said.

"What is it?"

"The ROCAL and the army are in the system. They're requesting a video conference."

"Oh!" I shouted. "I almost forgot. Patch them through. They won't believe what we've just experienced."

Vanessa then displayed the video conference on the front window. Two figures appeared, both cognioids.

"Good day, Captain," they said simultaneously.

"Good space, err…who am I talking to?"

"I'm Captain Anika Flinn," the first cognioid said in a female voice. She had the same dark red detailing as me, but her emblem was a capitalized M with a human fist in the background, signifying that she was from the military.

"And I'm professor Aedan Grant from ROCAL," the second cognioid said. His vessel had light purple detailing. His emblem was a capital R in front of what looked like a human cell, which was weird considering ROCAL specialized in alien life.

"That's a very unusual name there. Aedan," I said , trying to lighten the mood.

"It was generated by a computer, like most people's names."

"Sure. But anyway, I'm assuming you're here because of the message pod we sent?"

They nodded.

"You have any good news?" the professor asked.

"Hah!" I shouted sarcastically. "Not good at all, but

definitely huge news." I turned to Vanessa's hologram, "Vanessa?"

"Yes?" she asked.

"Send them the footage I uploaded to you."

"And send them mine as well," the lieutenant added.

"Got it."

"I have to say," the professor began, "it's very strange that we got a message pod from this system."

"Why's that?" I asked.

"Well, we've been getting anonymous messages the past year, all advising us to come to this uncharted system."

"I had the coordinates wrongfully uploaded into me as well," Vanessa said.

"My apologies for trying to mine an uncharted planet," I said.

"It's okay," Captain Flinn replied.

"Wait," I said. "You didn't act on those anonymous messages?"

"No," he said. "Nobody responds to anonymous messages, let alone follow their advice."

"Well," I said grimly, "you sure should have. You'll be surprised with whatever is living down there."

"Are they hostile?" Captain Flinn asked.

I didn't answer, silence falling over the room. How was I going to explain this to them?

"They have weapons as advanced as ours," the lieutenant said clearly, seeming to have pulled himself together, at least for the time being. "And they know the importance of our mind chips and what they might contain. If I were you, Captain Flinn, I'd send for backup, and I'd bring the best weapons that you possess in your arsenal. You know, the ones we miners know nothing about."

"You'll understand why he said that when you watch the footage," I added.

"Any casualties?"

"One dead. Two had their mind chips destroyed, but

are backed up.

"Who's the one that died?" the professor asked.

"Bobby Brooklyn. He wasn't backed up."

"How did he die?"

"I shot his chip," the lieutenant said.

They both went quiet for a moment, until the professor asked, "Why?"

"They were trying to get information out of it with one of their computers and I was running out of power. I didn't have any other option."

Another silence hit the room.

"We'll take it from here then," Captain Flinn said, breaking the awkward silence. "You guys can jump back to Earth. They already have some idea of the situation and will debrief you once you get there."

"If this isn't some weird ruse you cognioids planned out—which will get you in a lot of trouble, might I add—then this will make all of you very important in the coming time," the professor said.

I was shocked by what he said. I could tell by Vanessa's hologram that she was just as surprised as well, and not by the implication of our importance in this whole thing, but by the fact that he would even think that we'd fake something like this. My circuits were overheating with the anger that flowed through me. But before I could confront him, the lieutenant let his thoughts fly.

"Ruse!?" he asked angrily. "Are you fucking kidding me!? Do you know what the fuck we've been through!? I had to kill our recruit you incompetent bastard!"

"I-I-I was just—" the professor stuttered.

"I-I-I was just—" the lieutenant mocked him, "Get the fuck out of our ship."

"Well, I-I'm not in your ship."

"Just cancel the damn—"

And before he could finish his sentence Vanessa interrupted. "Captain!" she shouted.

"Yes, Vanessa?" I asked, unable to control the grin on my face.

"The results from one of the samples is back. A dark purple substance."

"That's the blood of one of the natives we shot," the lieutenant added.

"What does it say?" I asked.

"It has cells, with DNA packed in a nucleus."

"Interesting," the professor said.

"Why is that interesting?" I asked.

"Well, we never knew what the building blocks would be of alien life, DNA was on the list, but we figured it was likely something entirely different. Did you by any chance compare it to a human sample?"

"Yes, it's a sixty-seven percent match."

"A bit higher than you would think, but still interesting."

"That's not all," Vanessa continued.

"What is it?" I asked.

"It has mitochondrial DNA."

"What!?" the professor shouted. "That's impossible! I swear to you, if this is some kind of prank, it will have dire consequences for your crew!"

"Oh, you little—" Nate started.

"This isn't a joke professor," I cut in. "Why do you keep thinking that?"

"Because an alien life form made out of cells with nuclear DNA is already considered a miracle, but it having *mitochondrial* DNA? That's absurd! It defies everything we've researched and hypothesized at ROCAL."

"Did you match it to *our* mitochondrial DNA, Vanessa?" I asked.

"Yes, Captain. I just did. But I think we have to redo the tests before we can conclude anything."

"How much is it?"

"Captain, I really think we should redo the tests

before—"

"How much is it?" I repeated.

"Ninety-eight percent."

AUTHOR BIO

C. F. Harret writes

Contact information:
Email: cfharret@gmail.com
Instagram: @cfharret
Twitter: @c_harret

MY GRATITUDE

Thank you for supporting me by buying and reading this book.

If you liked it, please consider leaving a review on Amazon.com and Goodreads.com. It will help immensely with its success and writing a sequel to this story.

Scan me and leave a review

If you are interested in subscribing to my newsletter to be notified of future works.

Scan me and subscribe

www.ingramcontent.com/pod-product-compliance
Lightning Source LLC
LaVergne TN
LVHW041208150826
845673LV00001B/325

* 9 7 8 9 9 9 1 4 7 5 3 4 9 *